Y

Der
Derleth, August William, 1909-
1971.
Sweet land of Michigan

Sweet land of Michigan

DATE DUE

FE 24 7			
AP 77			

SWEET LAND OF MICHIGAN

Sweet Land of Michigan

By
AUGUST DERLETH

DUELL, SLOAN AND PEARCE
New York

First Edition

Affiliate of
MEREDITH PRESS
Des Moines & New York

Library of Congress Catalogue Card Number: 62-8533

MANUFACTURED IN THE UNITED STATES OF AMERICA

VAN REES PRESS • NEW YORK

CONTENTS

SWEET LAND OF MICHIGAN

I.

A VOLUNTEER FOR THE MILITIA

DAVID WAS IN the lean-to, forking hay to the horses, when he heard sounds from outside. He froze, thinking of Indians. But, no—Indians would never make that much noise. If they were coming to raid this lonely house in the clearing, they would come by stealth, in the night, and not betray themselves with the sounds of their coming. And it couldn't be Willie, he told himself. Willie was probably still in bed.

He held the fork tight and stepped outside. The lean-to was next to the east wall of the house. David went around it. There was still snow on the ground, but now that the middle of March had passed, much of the snow and ice had melted. The ground was still frozen.

There was someone on the road, on horseback. David stared, unbelievingly. The fellow was a soldier of some kind. And what would he be doing coming from the other direction, not from Detroit but from the woods on the west? A hard-riding man too. The horse looked tired and frozen mud reached almost half way up its legs. Come through the marshes, thought David. He had seen uniforms like this one in Detroit, but he could not remember now what kind of soldier the man might be.

He put down his fork and went toward the road. During the winter, few people passed by, and the road was scarcely marked at all. A preacher once in a while. And Indians. Hardly anybody else, unless Flem Gibson came to call from the west side, or Toddy Cobbett from the east. But they were miles off and hardly set foot outside their places unless their womenfolk were dying for somebody else to talk to and gave them no rest until they went visiting.

The fellow seemed to be almost asleep on his horse.

"Morning," said David in a loud voice.

The traveler sat up. He seemed to uncurl. His long arms shot out from his chest, his head came up, and altogether he looked suddenly a foot taller and two feet wider.

"Ha, a sprout!" he said in a voice that was half a growl. "Lt. Bell—Charlie Bell—of the Michigan Militia." He pulled his horse to a stop and leaned over his neck. "It's men we need. How many men here?"

"Two," answered David.

"And the place scarce big enough for one," said the lieu-tenant, casting his eye around. "Perhaps we can have the other."

He slid off the horse. He was neither as tall nor as big as

he looked. His horse stood docile, except for smelling at David. It's the hay he smells, David thought.

"Bring him along. I'll give him some hay."

"And I could do with a bit myself. Lead me to your men, Boy. And whose place is it I've come to?"

"Pa's name is John Claver. Mine's Dave."

"Well, thank ye, Davie. It's hard riding I've done. Spent the night at Gibson's, and set out again before dawn."

David pointed silently to the house. Then he took the horse around to feed it some hay. As quickly as he could, he returned to the house.

Lt. Bell had just finished introducing himself to John Claver. "Here's the one of the men," he said. "Now, where's the other?"

"Here," said David.

"Gulled!" exclaimed the lieutenant good-naturedly. "And by a sprout! How old are ye, Davie?"

"Seventeen."

"Ye're on the road early, Lieutenant," Pa said soberly. "Ye're not pleasure bent, I'm bound."

" 'Twould be a madness to be pleasure bound in March in this Territory of Michigan, sir," said Bell. "I'm on the Governor's business. See here."

He reached into his coat as he spoke and pulled out a folded paper. He unfolded it and put it down on the table before Pa. But his eyes were not looking at it, David saw. The lieutenant was looking at the fresh salt-rising bread Ma had brought out, and the stewed dried apples, and the ham.

David crowded forward and read the proclamation. It was written in large letters. "A Proclamation: To All Able-

Bodied Men of the Territory of Michigan. The Territorial Militia has an immediate need of volunteers to repel the enemy at our border. We ask you to report to headquarters in Detroit without delay, and be prepared to march . . ." David dropped his eyes to the signature: "Stevens T. Mason, Governor of the Territory of Michigan."

"What enemy?" demanded Pa.

"Man, it's not me does the saying. It's the Governor. I didn't stop to ask him. General Brown gave us orders, and we went out to carry the proclamation about the Territory. Been out all of ten days past. I'll be back in Detroit today, and so will we all if we're in luck."

"The Indians?" asked David.

Lt. Bell shrugged.

"I can't go," said Pa. "There's land to be cleared, land to be turned . . ."

A rising tide of excitement caught David. "I can," he said quickly. "Pa, let me go."

Silence fell in the room. Behind him, David heard Ma suck in her breath. Ma don't want me to go, he thought. Willie was looking at him in envy. Baby Joey was undecided whether to smile or cry. And Ginny watched curiously to see what Pa would say. As for Lt. Bell—he just looked at David and sort of grinned. He'd as lief I didn't go, thought David. This made him all the more determined.

"It's a question," said the lieutenant. "Can the boy use a gun?"

"There's no fear as to that," said Pa quietly. "He's a good shot. This far out in the woods, it don't pay not to be."

"Squirrels is different from men," said Bell.

"If there's to be a war," said Pa slowly, "it's a man's bounden duty to go—if he's able."

"I'd be more use to you in the militia than here, Pa," urged David.

The very uncertainty about the "enemy" confirmed David's desire to join up. The danger of Indians had always been there. Ever since David was twelve, since they had come by boat to Detroit and crossed overland to this place, Indians had menaced them. No one ever knew when they would turn from being friendly and become enemies, falling upon the little settlements to "take meat" and butcher the white man. So far it had not happened. Perhaps the time had come. Still, David reasoned, if it were the Indians, wouldn't the militia be asking the families to come into the nearest forts and garrisoned towns? Perhaps England was at war with the country again.

"Ye needn't decide this moment," said Lt. Bell. "There'll be a column marching by this way in a week or ten days, bound south. Ye can join us or not then, as ye see fit. I reckon there's room for sprouts as well as men."

David would have been offended, but there was a twinkle in the lieutenant's eye. He grinned.

"Will you join us at breakfast, Lieutenant?" asked Ma.

"Thank ye, Ma'am," Bell answered eagerly. "That I will."

The lieutenant moved quickly up to the table. Now that he knew his breakfast was only a moment away, he gave David a keen glance, measuring him. David met his eye and grinned again. Lt. Bell grinned back. David had already begun to like him. As for spending quite a while with him, now, on second thought, he was not sure he would like it. It was having to make a choice of Pa and Ma, Willie, Ginny and Joey—as well as Ned and Ben in the shed—on one hand, and the militia on the other.

For the first time, David realized that the excitement he foresaw with the militia was balanced by everything he would miss here at home—the new forty of trees to be girdled and cut down, the roots to be grubbed out to make more land for corn; the hay to be cut and stacked against winter; the spring-house to be kept clean; the cattle to be cared for; the rail fences to be kept up—and, most of all, the warm friendly evenings around the fireplace, and the rare visits of neighbors or of Preacher Sommers.

All this time Pa had said nothing. What was Pa thinking about? he wondered. His eyes were looking past the table, and, though Pa seemed to be gazing at him, David could see that he was looking past him, too.

"A week or ten days, ye say?" said Pa at last to Bell.

"About that time. Time enough so's the boy can do all the work he ought to get done before he takes off. Might be gone as much as a year. But, then—he won't be too far away."

"Are we in any danger here?" asked Pa.

"Don't spect so," said Bell shortly.

Pa was puzzled, David could see. If it were Indians, they would likely be coming in from the north or west. If the British, from the east, since they were right across from Detroit. What was on the south but Ohio? David was puzzled, too. The militia marching south! What could it mean? But Bell did not offer a word. Perhaps he had his orders and was only obeying them.

Pa did not want to ask any more. And David knew, if he went, he would find out soon enough. It was good now to know that Pa and Ma and the rest weren't in any danger.

Now Ma was getting ready to say grace. David bowed his head with the others.

In no time at all the days passed. Nine days later, at about noon, a column of men on horse and in wagons came along the crude wilderness road which passed in front of the Claver clearing. Willie heard them first. He and David were at work girdling trees when Willie heard the noise of their coming. David had been ready for five days.

Now he ran to the house, Willie following. He burst into the kitchen.

"They're coming, Ma," he cried. "I'll get my things."

"You're set on going, David?"

"Sure, Ma. But I'll come back some day—don't you worry none."

"Don't forget to read in books whenever you get the chance. And the Good Book, too." She turned to Willie, who stood on the threshold. "Willie, call Pa." Willie was off at once, and his mother turned again to David. "And learn to mind when you're told to do things, as long as you're doing right. It won't be as easy as it is at home where you're going."

"Yes, Ma."

David had got his knapsack from under the bed. He ran to the window for the first sight of the company of men he was to join. They were still behind the trees, but he could hear them singing raggedly, out of tune.

Willie came running back to the kitchen. "Pa's comin'," he said, and stood gazing at David. He was just about green with envy, thought David. He could already see David a militiaman, and he had all kinds of notions about the fun David was going to have. It was written all over his freckled face. It was a good thing Willie was almost fifteen, and old enough to help Pa just about as much as David had done.

"You get all my jobs, Willie," David said. "You come after Pa now."

"I know," said Willie. "Till you come back, Dave."

David heard a step outside. Pa's coming, he thought. Pa showed up in the doorway. They looked at each other steadily.

"So ye're really goin', Davie?"

"Yes, Pa."

"I been rovin' myself a long time. Ever since I was a boy. I never found any better land to settle on than this here land of Michigan. It's good land, comin' up fast."

"Yes, Pa."

Pa pointed to the door. "That door'll always be open to ye, Son. Be a good boy, and stay honest."

Willie, who had pushed forward to the window, turned and said excitedly. "Here they come now. Gosh, there's about hundreds of 'em. One of 'em's riding ahead."

David looked. There did seem to be over a hundred men. He could not see how many were in the wagons. The one riding ahead, he was glad to see, was Lt. Bell.

David took a tighter hold of his knapsack. Now, at this moment, he wished he were already on the way. He was afraid of what Ma might do. Ma might cry; that would make him feel bad. He felt bad enough already. He almost wished he had not made up his mind to leave. At first the excitement had won him, and then a more sober sense of duty. Most of all, he guessed, it was wanting to get away from the farm. Still, some of the men in the Territory would have to answer the Governor's appeal. Even if every household in the country sent a man into the militia, there might not be enough. There were not even a hundred thousand white people in the entire Territory of Michigan, counting all the women and children on both sides of Lake Michigan. Besides, most men and boys who lived outside the towns knew how to handle a gun. Some, like himself, were pretty good with bow and arrow, too.

For a moment no one moved or said anything. Then Ma came over and kissed him quick-like, on the cheek, and Pa clapped him on the shoulder and said, "I reckon a boy's a man before his Pa knows it." Ginny began to sniffle and Joey, seeing her tears, to howl. Willie said, "He's at the door."

Lt. Bell's knock fell on the door, and Willie went to open it.

The lieutenant's hearty voice preceded him into the house. "Do we have a recruit or has the boy changed his mind?" Then he saw them waiting for him. "Good day to you all. Ha! I see Davie's with us."

"I'm ready," said David.

"Has war started?" asked Pa.

Bell shook his head. "Not a shot's been fired yet. Nor like to be—at any rate, not soon. We've raised a force of nigh on to twelve hundred men to keep the border, and I figure that'll set anybody with a mind to invading us to think twice. We'd best get on. We're to meet General Brown and the rest of the men tomorrow noon."

Lt. Bell promised Pa and Ma that he would look after David, that chances were no harm would come to him, since he looked to be a sharp lad, and they were not to worry. David could see that Pa was itching to ask again about the enemy, and would have, had he not known that the lieutenant would put him off again. It was both sad and funny to see the baffled expression on Pa's face. What Ma thought was plain in her eyes. If the lieutenant had not been there, she would be sniffling and crying along with Ginny.

Soon they were out of the house and going down toward the road. Another horse was tied up there beside the lieutenant's.

"I figured you'd likely know this country a little better'n I'd remember it. So you'll ride up ahead with me till we're further along and picking up somebody who'll know it better there," explained Bell. "Then you can ride in the wagon. We ain't got enough horses to go around yet. But they do promise us enough guns. Should of told you to fetch yours."

"Pa'll need it."

"Reckon he will."

David mounted the horse. It was a bony-backed nag, no longer young, and underfed, too. Bell raised his hand in farewell to the family gathered before the house. David looked back. He had a sinking feeling. For one wild moment he thought of jumping off the horse and running back to stay with them at home, but he fought it down. He forced a grin he did not feel, shouted "Good-bye, Pa! Good-bye, Ma!" and waved.

Then he turned and followed Lieutenant Bell.

II.

SOUTH TOWARD OHIO

THE COLUMN of men and wagons had gone on ahead. They were no longer singing, but they made enough noise to make up for that. David guessed they had hit one of the soft places, of which there were a great many. They would have a time getting the wagons through. March was almost over, and the thaw had set in so much that the road in many places was just muck, with deep ruts and water holes in it.

They caught up with the column. Lt. Bell, with an eye for the higher, more solid ground, rode around it. David followed. Bell shouted his scorn at the men who had mired a wagon. Then they were at the head of the column, and the lieutenant fell back to let David take the lead.

The jostling of a wagon could hardly have been worse

than the bony nag he rode, thought David. If he had to ride him very long, he would be sore all over. Futhermore, the horse was not used to this kind of terrain, just as if he had been kept in a compound most of his life. Probably he was one of the horses from Fort Dearborn. David had all he could do to guide him where he wanted him to go. Luckily, they need not go very fast, for the column behind could not keep up if they did.

At the little knoll a half mile from home, David turned once more. From here he could just see home through an open place among the treetops. Someone was still standing in the yard, knowing the column would be visible at this place where the crude road led over a rise in the land. It was Ma. David made an arc with his cap in his hand. He could see the white fluttering of her apron. Pa and Willie had gone back to their work. They'll get along, David told himself, even though Pa'll miss me. It made him feel good to know that they would miss him as much as he would miss them.

Lt. Bell rode up.

"We'll turn to the south at the next crossing," he said.

"But that's only an Indian trail!" protested David. "We'll have to chop a way through for the wagons some places."

"That don't matter. That's the way we go. We'll be meeting General Brown and more of the men in the south."

The Indian trail crossed the settlers' road about a mile past Gibson's place. David half expected Ned Gibson to come out and join the column, too, but they did not stop at the Gibson house. David was disappointed. He had seen mighty few young faces among the column of men when he rode past; he had hoped there would be more "sprouts", as Lieutenant Bell had called him.

David tried to guess where they were going. "South" meant Ohio. If they had set out from Detroit that morning, it would be about noon when they got to Pa's place. Ten miles or so, maybe less. About noon next day, the column was to meet General Brown and most likely the main body of the militia, come down from Detroit. That would be nearly half way to Ohio.

At least, they would be out of the wilderness.

A mile after taking the turn—and one of their slowest miles, for they had to stop twice to widen the road for the wagons—David gave his lead to Lieutenant Bell. The men were now moving into country strange to David. He did not know what lay to the south, though he recognized that they moved slowly in toward the lake shore, which curved into the southwest in that direction. David had traveled widely in the country near his home. But, since they had come to the Michigan Territory in 1830, five years before, neither David nor anyone else in his family had been farther back along that route from the east than Fort Dearborn.

When the lieutenant took over the head of the column once more, David fell back into the column. At first he stayed up near the head of it. Then he moved gradually farther and farther back until he found himself abreast of another volunteer who could not have been much older than he was. The other was just as curious about David as David was about him. The two of them, riding side by side, eyed each other, taking each other's measure for a few minutes before either one spoke.

"I'm Dave Claver," said David at last.

"Nate Pendleton's my name," said the other. "Saw you come in. I'm from Detroit."

His voice was warm and friendly. He spoke easily. His face was good-natured. He had a row of freckles high across his nose and cheeks. His eyes were brown and sharp-looking. His mouth was wide, and it was easy for him to smile. David took a liking to him right away, and he could see that Nate didn't mind riding alongside him.

"Where we going?" David asked then.

"Wish I could tell you," answered Nate. "All I know there's some kind of fooferaw going on down toward Ohio. No shooting so far. But somebody's making big muscles at us, and we're going down to make muscles back."

David laughed. "You been long in Detroit?" he asked.

Nate shook his head. "About a year. Come in from Rhode Island. We got a big family, and I figure Pa and Ma didn't mind much when I joined up. They got enough to feed as it is."

"Did they want you to go?" asked David, wonderingly.

Nate shrugged. "Oh, I guess it wasn't just that way. They didn't tell me to join up—nothing like that. I just went and did it. I been to school some. How about you?"

"I guess not as much as you," admitted David. "But Ma taught me to read and write evenings. We got some books, and I've read the whole Bible, end to end."

"Well, that makes up for a lot of schooling—all that reading," said Nate. "Never did learn much about reading myself." He looked at David shrewdly and guessed his age. "Seventeen?"

"You're not much older."

"Just turned eighteen," said Nate.

Somehow, as they talked together and got to know something about each other, David was less lonesome. He had been starting to feel just a little homesick—not because he was gone from home, but because it might be a long time before he would see his folks again. Now that feeling was gone. He felt he had a new friend in Nate.

They rode together for all of two miles.

Then Lt. Bell came riding back, bawling, "Nate Pendleton. Come up ahead!"

Nate dug his heels into his horse and rode up. After that, David dropped back just about to the end of the column.

They seemed to be coming out of the densest wilderness now. David was surprised to see how many farms there were. When Pa and Ma and the rest of them came out from Detroit only five years before, they had seen hardly anybody but Indians. Then Gibsons moved in—two years ago—after Cobbetts, who had been there a year longer. But here, south of where they lived, less than five miles south, there were more places. The Indian trail here was widened out into something more like a road. It was very muddy, and sometimes the sink-holes delayed the whole column almost as much as chopping down trees to make the trail wide enough for the wagons had done back further.

More volunteers joined the column in this part of the country, too. Most of them were older than David. They were young men in their twenties. No wonder, thought David —the country had three times as many settlers as that land west of Detroit. Most likely they'd be heading into still more settled places before the column of marching men reached the border of Ohio.

Not long before the column struck camp for the night, Nate came back to where David was.

"I figure you don't like farming, Dave," he said, as he fell in at his side.

David hesitated before answering. "I don't know," he said truthfully. "Maybe I don't. Maybe it's just because I've never been anywhere or seen anything else. I like to help my folks —but I've got a hankering to do something else."

"Now, me, I guess I'd just as soon farm as anything," confided Nate.

"You!" exclaimed David in astonishment.

"Sure. I don't like it much in town. Figure I'd just as soon be working the land as anything. A man'll never starve on a farm, and he's his own boss, too. After you work around a little, Dave, you'll find out it's not so much fun working for somebody else unless you make up your mind to swallow a lot."

Nate's talk started David thinking. Why had he been so quick to volunteer? It wasn't just the promise of excitement, though it was true the quiet life he led palled on him now and then. It wasn't just the hope of seeing something of the world. It certainly wasn't to get out of all the spring work on Pa's place. Maybe it was that he wanted to prove to himself that he could go out on his own. Was it partly because he didn't like farming? He did not think so. He had never said a word of how he felt to Pa because he did not know how to say it. Maybe Pa had guessed.

"Ain't you been fed good and treated right, Son?" Pa had asked him one day during that time they were waiting for the militia to come for him.

David had been quick to admit that he had. "But farming ain't everything," he had said.

"That's so," Pa had answered. "But it's the backbone of

the country. It keeps a man and his family. It lets a man be next to where the grass and the corn grow, where he can hear the birds sing, and feel the earth around him."

It was the longest speech Pa had ever made, but David had neither denied it nor accepted it. And Pa had not asked him again why he wanted to join up. Perhaps he knew David wanted to get out on his own.

That night, when they stopped to camp, they built three big roaring bonfires. The night would be cold, and the column of men carried only blankets in the wagons with the food for the men. Some of the men were detailed to gather more wood and keep the fires going, while the rest stretched out in a circle around the fires, wrapped in blankets. David and Nate were among the wood-gatherers for the first half of the night.

For all that the woods loomed black all around, there were more clearings to be seen, more tight little log cabins, with hay-cocks along one side of the houses, and sometimes cattle sheds and stalls for horses, and once or twice even pig-pens and chickens. There were more fences and more people, and David knew, if he had had doubt any longer, that whoever it was they were coming up to fight, it wasn't the Indians. They'd have gone north and west for that, not south, where there were so many white people. So it must be other white men, he thought, and that puzzled him all the more.

There was little time to talk or stand around for the first half of the night. The wood detail had to hustle constantly, because the big fires devoured a lot of wood. David and Nate were exhausted when at last their turn came to sleep.

How different it all was! thought David, as he lay rolled up in a blanket of his own, with Nate already asleep beside him. The men lay all around, and the bonfires cast an orange glow over everyone. Out past the circle of the bonfire light lay the darkness, and high overhead shone the stars, many of which David could name. The Heavenly Hunter hung just off his shoulder, low in the southwest sky. High up the east shone the amber star Pa always called the Spring-Bringer, though its name was Arcturus.

He thought of Pa and Ma. They would be sleeping half the night already now. He wished he could just see them. It was David's first night away from his family, his first night spent in any other place but home. Each night now would be away from home. Just as there was a world of difference between last night and this so there would be difference now from one night to the next.

He closed his eyes tight, and whispered the same prayer he had been taught at his mother's knee years before. In a little while he slipped into sleep.

Early in the afternoon of the next day, Lt. Bell's column caught up with the main body of the militia. They were moving slowly southward. Lt. Bell's column had reached the place of meeting two hours late, and General Brown had pushed on. Seeing all the men ahead of them, David felt even more a part of something important about to happen.

"Look," cried Nate, as they drew closer to the troops ahead, "there's General Brown." He pointed.

The General was a stocky man. At the approach of Lt. Bell's column, he had detached himself from a slender young man who rode at his side, and ridden back to ride up and down the new column, measuring the volunteers. He had a sharp, almost piercing glance, and a gruff manner, but he looked more military than anyone else in the column, including Lt.

Bell. He paused briefly opposite David and Nate. Lt. Bell came up anxiously behind him. The General wheeled on him.

"You were late, Bell."

"Sir, we had to cut our way through the forest in three places and get unstuck of the mud in two others."

General Brown merely grunted.

From the front of the main body of militiamen, the slender young man rode out. He came half way up toward the General and paused, seeing that General Brown had moved back a little from the new column and was about to speak to them.

"Men," the General said in a loud voice, commanding instant silence. "We'll continue the march without any more delay. By late tomorrow, we ought to arrive at the battle line, barring any unforeseen accidents. If we're delayed by any tomfoolery, we'll march by night. Do you understand me?"

"Yes, sir," answered Lt. Bell for his men.

General Brown turned and rode back toward the head of the militia. The slender young man, who David thought must be someone important, fell in again at his side.

"Battle line?" repeated David, looking at Nate.

Nate raised his eyebrows and shrugged. "Can't be a battle," he said sensibly. "Or he'd be there with the militia, wouldn't he?"

Lt. Bell came riding along the column, shouting savagely. "All right, now, men. Let's all straighten up. Let's try to look like soldiers. Get a move on!"

The column began to move south once more.

III.

THE SETTLEMENT AT THE BORDER

AT EVENING of the following day the militia reached a settlement. It was a village of some size, not, of course, as big as Detroit, nor nearly as bustling as Detroit would be when the lakes opened up and the settlers would be coming in again through the port, as they did every spring. David had no idea where they were, but, by looking around past the houses and seeing an ice-covered stream, and, further east, what appeared to be a lake, he reasoned that they were somewhere along Lake Erie, south of Detroit. At this point, the lake lay in toward the river, forming a long bay.

As they listened to the talk of the men around them, David and Nate grew more perplexed than ever. Some said they were at the settlement of Toledo. Others insisted they were at Port

Lawrence or Swan Creek. Not until Lt. Bell came in among the men to tell them that General Brown would speak to the militia as soon as they had eaten their evening meal was the puzzle solved. All three places were the same. Port Lawrence and Swan Creek were only older names for Toledo. So they were at Toledo on the banks of the Maumee River, and the long bay was Maumee Bay.

"Here we stay," said Bell without further explanation.

David and Nate wondered where the hostiles were. No one else, however, appeared to be concerned. The men of the militia sat around their small campfires and laughed and joked, as if they had not a care in the world. They had been told to stay here and they were content to stay.

Before long, gossip drifted among the men. It was hard to believe. A grizzled militiaman of thirty or so brought it to where David and Nate sat. He leaned over them, his little eyes gleaming in the firelight.

"We're fixin' to fight Ohio," he said. "You heard?"

"What for?" demanded Nate.

"Fact. You'll see," he said, and went on.

"Ohio's Americans," said David.

"It's just talk," Nate was confident.

David was not so sure. He had wondered all along about whom they were to stand against. He had told himself it couldn't be Indians, and it wasn't likely to be the British. Only other Americans were left.

They were not left long in doubt. A bugler blew assembly and the men crowded around a makeshift platform on which General Brown waited to talk to them. The platform had torches stuck into each corner. The flickering light from the flames reddened General Brown's face and made him look half roasted. When the men were all gathered together, he began to talk.

"Men, we're in Toledo. Our job is to hold this place. The State of Ohio has laid claim to a strip of land about eight miles wide at this end, tapering off to five miles on the west, and a hundred miles long. According to the Fulton survey, this land belongs to the Territory of Michigan. According to their Harris survey, it belongs to the State of Ohio. It can't be both. Ohio has laid claim to it as of last month, and we're reliably told they're moving up troops.

"We got here first, as we meant to do. Governor Mason and I doubt very much that they'll dare to move on Toledo as long as we're here. So we stay here. Some of you will keep to such lodgings as we can provide. Others will be billeted among the citizens of this city. Weapons will be issued to all who don't already own them. So will other supplies a militia-man ought to have. I want to add that those of you who want to send letters home may do so tomorrow morning with a party riding back to Detroit. We'll make every effort to see to it that the people at home learn where you are. That's all."

The men gave the General an uncertain cheer. Then they began to disperse.

"I'm going to write my folks," said David, "if I can get hold of ink and paper."

"They'll not be plentiful, I'll be bound," said Nate.

The two of them immediately set out in search of paper, pen and ink. Their search led them to Lt. Bell. The lieutenant guessed that 'there might be some such supplies with General Brown. He cocked an eye at them.

"You boys figurin' to write home?" he asked.

"Yes, sir," answered Nate.

"I'd be obliged to ye if ye'd set down a few lines for me. My handwriting's worse than hen's scratchin'."

"Glad to," said David.

"And me, too," said another of the men, who was standing by and had overheard.

"I guess we're in business, Nate."

"Reckon we are."

"I'll get ye what ye need," promised the lieutenant. "Find yourselves something to write on and wait for me."

In less than an hour, David and Nate were busy writing letters. It was surprising how many of the men who crowded around could not write at all, or with such labored effort that none wanted to try. They wrote their own letters first. David made his as long as he could. Then he wrote a short letter for Lt. Bell.

The men who crowded forward wanted some word sent to their families, too, but when either David or Nate asked them what they wanted to say, most of them did not know, or simply told the boys to write that they were in Toledo and were safe, there was no fighting, and might not be any.

Lt. Bell had brought a quantity of rough, discolored paper, pen and ink, and sealing wax. Each letter had to be folded and sealed. Lt. Bell collected them on the spot. If they were for Detroit, they went free, because they would be taken right to the post office. If they were for outside of Detroit, each letter cost two bits.

While they were busy writing, David was suddenly aware that the men drew back a little, as silence fell on the group. He looked up. There, standing not far away, watching them, was the slender young man he had seen at a distance the day before with General Brown. He was handsome, but also haughty, in the way he looked at them. He was dressed like a dandy—with a black frock coat over a black silk vest, a white shirt, and a black tie. His high forehead, with dark hair brushed bushily down both sides of his head, made him look taller than the men. He had high eyebrows, wide-set eyes, and a small, stubborn mouth over a narrow, sharp chin, though the upper part of his face was broad. What was even worse, he carried a cane, though he did not seem to be lame. David's long stare did not abash him in the least; indeed, he smiled a little.

Then he turned from the boys and beckoned to Lt. Bell.

The lieutenant went over to him in a hurry and listened without a word while the other spoke to him. He did not answer, other than to nod—and how obediently! thought David. Surely, whoever the slender young man was, he was somebody with authority who could make even General Brown jump!

Lt. Bell came back and said, "As soon's you finish, General Brown wants to see the both of you."

"Who was that fellow?" David asked Nate, when Bell had stepped back.

Nate shrugged. "Seen him around Detroit now and then. Don't know his name, though."

Long before they were finished, Lt. Bell was urging them to hurry and get done. "Can't keep General Brown waiting," he said. "Ye can do the rest when ye get back. I don't expect a man like the General'll have much to say to ye."

"We'll see," said David.

"Sure. Maybe he wants our advice about how to end the war," added Nate, grinning.

"Ha! a fine war it'd be if the General'd have to ask a couple of boys—hardly dry behind the ears—how to run it!" said Bell scornfully. "Come on, now. I'll take ye where he is."

Lt. Bell strode forward. The two boys followed.

"You know what?" whispered David to Nate. "I don't believe the General's asking after us. I think it's that other fellow."

"Might be," agreed Nate. "But what for?"

"We'll find that out."

They took long steps and fell in beside Lt. Bell.

"Mind ye listen—don't talk," growled the lieutenant. "Never open yer mouth till ye've got something to say."

General Brown's headquarters were a short distance removed from the militia. The men were crowded into the settlement from the north end, almost to the middle, not counting the sentries who had been posted along the south edge of town and further up along the Maumee River. General Brown stayed in a private house just past the central part of Toledo. There was a sentry on duty at the front door, and no doubt another at the back. A square lantern hung beside the front door. Its light fell on a door-frame ornamented with fancy carving done by hand. There was even a little roof over the front stoop. Two steps led up to the door.

Lt. Bell was let in. He vouched for the boys. Then he stepped squarely into the room where General Brown waited. He began to talk at once.

"General, sir, here's the boys. This one's David Claver—" saying which, he reached behind him and pushed David forward—"and this one's Nate Pendleton." Nate came into the room ahead of Bell's propelling hand.

The moment David could catch Nate's eye, he grinned. There, sure enough, was the slender young man with the haughty look who had been watching them write letters. General Brown sat at a table covered with a red checkered cloth. This was at the far wall of the room. The young man stood in the middle of the room, with his legs spread out a little, and his hands clasped behind him.

"That's all, Lieutenant. You may go," said General Brown.

Lt. Bell flashed a glance of warning at the boys—as if to tell them to watch their tongues and not speak out of turn —together with a faint smile. Then he excused himself and left.

General Brown spoke again. "Boys, you may not have the privilege of knowing the Honorable Stevens Mason, Governor of the Territory of Michigan."

So that's who he is! thought David. No wonder he could order even General Brown around if he had a mind to. Oh, but he was a dandy! Now he was walking back and forth, looking the boys over as if they were cattle on the market. Then he came up a little closer and began to talk.

"Come ahead, boys, come ahead. At ease. I saw you working so industriously tonight."

"Yes, sir," said David. Nate nodded.

"I like to see enterprise in young people."

Young people! David almost smiled. Why, the Governor himself wasn't much more than in his twenties, and not far in at that, if he were any judge.

"So few of your people know how to write," the Governor went on. "A pity, but true. I suppose they have to work too hard to make a living in the wilderness to take any time studying. Everything else always comes second to making a living. But you two, at least, have combined work with learning." He made a quick, impatient movement of his hands, while behind him General Brown leaned forward, his face growing tense with interest and curiosity. "But I didn't send for you to talk about that, did I, now?"

He went right on, not waiting for anyone to answer his question. "I don't doubt you heard General Brown this evening. You know why we're here. I don't think there'll be any bloodshed, but I issued the order to hold Toledo and prevent Governor Lucas of Ohio and his troops from entering the area of Maumee Bay. Just the same, I don't know how the people of Toledo feel about it. Some for, some against—granted. I'd like to have a better idea. I need some sharp ears to help me find out. I'd guess a couple of boys like you could get out and mix around with people without being much suspected of being soldiers. You don't look like the rest of the men. That's not to say you wouldn't make soldiers—only to suggest that you might like to find out for us what the people are saying, and not be taken for soldiers while you're doing it."

"You mean spying?" asked Nate bluntly.

"In a manner of speaking, yes."

Nate flashed a glance at David. The question in his eyes was in David's, too. But there was also a quickening of interest.

"You mean just go out and keep our ears open and let you know what we hear?" asked David. "And who said it?"

"Yes—and no. I'm not interested in who said it. I just want to know how many are for Michigan and how many for Ohio. There'll be plenty of talk in the morning, now we've come.

Once they find out that Ohio has about eight hundred men at Fort Miami—that's not far away—they'll be talking plenty. I want to know what they say. But I'm not interested in getting after anybody for his ideas on that subject."

"That's an order, men," interrupted General Brown.

The Governor turned to him patiently. "Gently, General —I'd far sooner have the boys make the decision."

General Brown snorted. The Governor turned casually to face David and Nate again. "Of course," he began, "if you'd rather not . . ." Then he paused.

"As for me," said David, "I'd just as soon try my hand at it."

"The same goes for me," added Nate quickly.

"Perhaps not together, boys. Two of you together are likely to excite more suspicion than either one alone—and if the people guess you're militiamen, you'll get only the side of the story they think you want to hear. That won't do us much good, will it?" He shook his head emphatically.

"Now, then," he went on, "if you're to go about this business in the morning, you won't want to be seen with the militia. Nor had you ought to stay here. I'd suggest you return to your camp, get your belongings, and go into the south end of the city. Take lodgings separately. General Brown will see to it that you get Conduct and will be free to go and come as you like.

"Then, tomorrow night, come to see us here after dark— unless, of course, Lucas is fool enough to march on Toledo. In that case, report back to your command at once. During the day, mix among the people—go to the shops, the taverns, the smithies—and listen to what they say. It's not hard work, you'll grant, and you're not likely to lose your heads even if they suspect you. Now, then, is that clear, boys?"

"Yes, sir," David and Nate answered together.

"Very well, then. General—?"

But General Brown was already scribbling rapidly at their passes.

IV.

A MISSION FOR THE GOVERNOR

O N THEIR WAY BACK to camp for their things, David said,
"I'd never figured he was the Governor!"

"He don't look like a Governor, and that's a fact," agreed
Nate.

"Still, you got to like him. He looks like a dandy, but he's
got his wits about him. He's sharp. When he talks, you know
what he means to say."

The money the Governor had given them jingled in their
pockets.

"I don't know as to the sense of what he wants us to do,"
said Nate. " 'Pears to me he could come right out and ask the
people. 'Tain't treason, no matter which way they decide.
Anyways, I reckon it won't be either one—our own Governor

or Lucas—who decides the whole thing. They'll decide it down in Washington."

"Unless they can settle it here first."

"What's all the fuss about, anyway?"

David could not say. He could guess. Perhaps Ohio wanted Maumee Bay. Perhaps Ohio just wanted Toledo and the people in that strip of land. Any way you looked at it, it wasn't much land, the way land lay all around, just waiting for settlers—a hundred miles across, by five at one end, and eight at the other. Marching men down to Toledo from Detroit, and up to Fort Miami from the capital of Ohio— wherever that was—seemed an all-fired fool thing to do.

Both boys decided at last that maybe Michigan Territory needed the count of the people in Toledo so that there'd be enough for Michigan to join the Union as a new State. That seemed the most likely explanation. Next to Detroit, Toledo was the biggest settlement around, and there had been talk in the Territory about joining up as a new State.

They got their knapsacks and walked back into the city. They had not gone far before David came to a halt under a spreading old maple tree.

"Reckon we'd better separate, don't you, Nate?" he asked.

"Guess so," agreed Nate. "Better plan to meet someplace, though."

"How about right here?"

"Good as any place."

"Tomorrow night then, just after dark."

The boys separated. David went one way, Nate another.

As he walked along, David kept his eyes open for a likely place to lodge for the night. He had fully expected to spend another night in camp. Yet here he was on his way to yet a different kind of adventure. It was certainly a contrasting life he led—and in so few days! He was on his own now, with a vengeance. He was proud, too, that he had been chosen by Governor Mason to be sent on this special mission, even if it was just a kind of spying. But at the same time, he could not help thinking how at this hour the robins would be singing in the clearing at home, and the meadowlarks would be hunting in the grasses. When he looked back from this street in Toledo, the little farm west of Detroit seemed no longer so isolated, no longer such a lonely place.

Toledo was still wide awake.

It was now well past sundown, and lights burned in almost every house. Word of the arrival of the Michigan militia had spread through town. Very likely now everybody was talking about it, thought David. It was probably the most exciting thing that had happened in Toledo since the Indians had moved away. The houses were all pressed up close to the roads, and the roads were all muddy. The night was not cold enough to harden the ground underfoot, and David had to walk with care lest he get his shoes muddy and make himself unwelcome wherever he might ask for room.

He walked to the south end of Toledo and began to look around for a place to stay. He meant to ask for but a single night's lodging, since he was confident that he and Nate could get a good idea of what people were saying in one day, and next night they would be back among the men. But the first place he tried turned him away; there was a houseful of boys and girls, and no room for anyone else. The second place, though, was a tidy little house with a fence around it, and here he was welcome, for it was owned by an old lady, a widow, who said her name was Matilda Wherry, and who made a great show of being glad to have someone she could talk to.

"Where ye bound fer?" she asked, her eyes curious.

"I'm headin' north," David answered.

"Ye're like to git into trouble," said the old woman, nodding her greying head gravely. "Here's all them Michiganders down in these parts ready to fight, and I hear tell as how the Ohioans are comin' up from below. My! I do wish they'd get that boundary settled between 'em, so's I can live in Ohio. The climate of Michigan never did agree with me."

David thought she was joking, but no, she was not. There was not a smile on her lips; she was just as serious as she could be. He had all he could do to keep from laughing out loud. In the first place, the old woman, who wore a sunbonnet in the house, was funny to look at. In the second, she was even more funny to listen to, for she went on talking about Michigan Territory and the State of Ohio just as if there was a lot of difference between them, as if Toledo were way down at the other end of Ohio, along the southern boundary, instead of the north. One thing and another were wrong with Michigan, but there was mighty little wrong with Ohio, according to her. So by the time he got to sleep, David figured on one sure partisan of Ohio to report to Governor Mason.

Next morning he was up early. The old lady was up before him. He had a little breakfast of salt pork and a kind of gruel, with some weak tea made from roots or leaves he was sure Mrs. Wherry had gathered herself, for it had a bitter taste, like some of the home-made tea Ma used to give him as medicine.

"I hoped you'd be up soon," she said, "because I'm anxious to get out and about and find out what them Michiganders look like."

"I reckon they're no different from other men," said David. "It's not as if they were foreigners."

When David left the house, he headed for the central part of town, where the shops and taverns were. It was scarcely eight o'clock, and the sun had come up not long before; yet there were already knots of people gathered on the streets and at the shops. David idled along with his ears wide. Nobody paid any attention to him. With his knapsack in his hand, he looked like any other of them, except that he seemed newly come into the settlement. Every little while he paused casually within earshot of groups of people who were talking too excitedly to notice him.

From time to time, he overheard snatches of conversation.

"Why'n't they go somewhere's else to fight? First thing we know they'll have us all on fire, and what'll we be to Michigan or Ohio then?"

"It's not Toledo they want, nor us—we don't count . . ."

"I'll stay where I was put, and I was put in Michigan before Ohio come along and laid claim to this part of the land."

"I was with Fulton's survey, and he was right—this is Michigan land!"

"Ye got rights in a State like Ohio—ye ain't got many rights in a Territory like Michigan. I'll take Ohio."

So it went most of the day, no matter where David stopped. Sometimes he took part in the discussion, but most of the time he just listened. Nobody minded his standing nearby. David guessed it wouldn't have mattered to them if he had been in the uniform of the militia, which wasn't very different from the homespun clothing most of the people wore.

It was the same in the few stores and taverns, except that there were no women in the taverns. Over all the people was a cloud of excitement. No matter how they felt—whether for Michigan or for Ohio—they were excited because the militia had come, and the only thing they worried about was not which would win, State or Territory, but whether their homes were in danger of being set on fire if there should be shooting. By and large, the talk of the people was just as funny as Mrs. Wherry's had been.

Nobody knew anything about the way the argument began. One group of men in one of the stores seemed to know why Ohio wanted Toledo—because of a canal the State was planning to build up from the Wabasa River to come out either on the Maumee River or the bay. A great many men were sure that Michigan had prior land rights to the whole area, including Toledo, because of an earlier survey. Another group of talkers standing on the board walk before a tavern insisted that Governor Mason needed the people of the disputed area to add to those of the Territory in order to swell the population to the point where it would be easier to demand the admission of Michigan to the Union of States.

Toledo was a small enough settlement so that it was easy to catch sight of Nate now and then. David saw him three times, once close enough to wink at him, but they did not speak until they came together at the place where they had agreed to meet, before returning to the quarters shared by Governor Mason and General Brown. When they met, it was already after dark.

They immediately compared notes. David told about Mrs. Wherry, laughing heartily when he remembered what she had said.

Nate laughed, too. "I was in a house where three men lived, with the wife of one of them," said Nate then. "They were all for Michigan. All they did was talk down Ohio. But it wasn't because they were really strong for Michigan. No, it was just because they heard about some canal Ohio was proposing to build, and they got to figurin' it would cost time and money to build it, and taxes would go up—so they'd sooner take a chance with Michigan!"

"I guess people are the same all over."

"Pretty much, I reckon."

The day had been a revelation to David as well as to Nate. How much people talked, and how little they really knew! Not that either of them knew very much about their reason for being there. And how many had Nate found for Michigan —and how many for Ohio? Why, no more than David, and no more for one side than the other.

The Governor and General Brown were waiting for them.

But David had hardly confronted Governor Mason than he guessed the Governor was off on another tack. Something else was gnawing away at him now; it was plain in Mason's handsome young face. It could be seen in the way he stalked up and down, clasping and unclasping his hands behind his back, his brow furrowed, and his lips pressed together.

The Governor listened to David and Nate, nodding his head to show that he followed all they said. General Brown threw in a comment from time to time, as much as to say, "I told you so."

"Then the fact is, as you judge it," said the Governor when

they had finished, "the people won't much care which way the matter goes."

"They're half one mind, half the other," said David. "I couldn't be honest and say they were more for Michigan than they are for Ohio."

"Nor me," added Nate. "Except they're worried about a battle that might set fire to the town."

"Good. Then we needn't expect any trouble from them. We'll not fire the town, and I doubt that Lucas will. But the fact is, we don't *know* what Lucas is up to. We suspect he's at Perrysburgh. I have some intelligence that there are two commissioners from Washington with Lucas. If so, we must be prepared to act."

"Our men are ready, sir," said General Brown stiffly.

Governor Mason looked vexed. "Softly, softly, General— any action we take against representatives of Ohio who try to act in an official capacity here must be taken by the sheriff of Lenawee County of Michigan Territory. A civil action, General—*not* a military one. We must take care that we don't put Washington on Ohio's side.

"I'm afraid statehood for Michigan depends on the admission of another slave state at the same time. So we'd better make haste slowly—if at all."

He stood for a long minute looking from one to the other of the boys. He seemed to be weighing them. David knew very well what he had in mind. He resolved not to wait for him to say it; he would say it himself first.

"How far away is Fort Miami, sir?"

"It's not Fort Miami we want. Only the troops are there. I'd suspect Lucas and his officers are at Perrysburgh."

"Then how far is Perrysburgh?"

"Reasonably nearby. Less than a day away. Perrysburgh isn't far, either, from Fort Miami—so Lucas can be in touch with the men encamped there on his orders."

"If we could get a horse, sir," began Nate.

But the Governor shook his head. "Anyone coming on horseback from the north would likely excite their suspicions right away. No, the best we could do would be to take you to within walking distance of Perrysburgh, and arrange to meet you again on another night."

"Wouldn't that be awkward, sir?" asked David quietly. "I used to track deer and fox at home—and you'd never get close to one that way."

Governor Mason grinned. "Just the same—it's too far to expect you to walk."

"Sir, couldn't we ride into Perrysburgh, present ourselves to Governor Lucas, and offer him information about our militia?"

General Brown let out a strangled snort and shouted, "Treason!"

Governor Mason eyed David thoughtfully. He stood there with one arm still behind his back. With his other hand, he stroked his chin. His eyes were narrowed, and his mouth pursed. He teetered back and forth on the balls of his feet.

"Be still, General," he said. "That we have twelve hundred men is information I don't mind Lucas knowing. That we intend to hold Toledo—likewise. What other way would be as easy for one of us to get near enough to Lucas to find out anything of his plans? This is just such outrageous folly as might succeed better than any other means we could think of. But two of you aren't necessary for this."

"No, sir," agreed Nate.

"That leaves you, David. Bear these facts in mind—Ohio's claim is based on the fact that civil elections under the laws of Ohio were held in Toledo and nearby in this disputed area. If you pose as a resident of the area, you'd know this, and your application to Lucas now must be made under the pretense of loyalty to Ohio. You'll want a horse, but none with a military look to him."

David grinned. "The nag I rode most of the way down here was just such a horse, sir."

"You shall have him. Now, then, you'll need some sleep. There's nothing urgent about this—you won't have to set out by night. Daylight will do as well for such a bold venture as yours!"

V.

DAVID BLUFFS THE ENEMY

Dᴀᴠɪᴅ ʀᴏᴅᴇ ɪɴᴛᴏ Perrysburg in the middle of the next morning.

He had set out before dawn, just in case someone might be in Toledo acting as a spy for the Ohio forces and might see him leaving the house in which Governor Mason and General Brown were quartered. Perrysburgh was up the Maumee River not quite ten miles from Toledo. It was on the south bank at that place where the Maumee widened out, well above the juncture with Swan Creek. It was the first settlement beyond Toledo.

David had enjoyed his journey very much. The way led through settled country. It reminded him of home, though there were more cleared areas and more farms. The road, except for being muddy, for it was now April, was well used. And the Maumee, beside which the road wound its way, was high and swollen with thaw water. In several places David had to make detours to avoid inlets of water—just as at home he had to avoid the sinkholes of the marshy areas.

Perrysburgh was almost as large as Toledo. Its streets were just about as muddy as Toledo's. Pigs and chickens made themselves at home all over. The pigs refused to move from the streets, but the chickens flew up, squawking, when David rode past, looking all around him for signs of the militia.

He decided that boldness would serve him best; so he stopped beside the first man he saw and asked where he could find Governor Lucas. But the old fellow did not know; he had heard that the Governor was in town, but he had no idea where. David thanked him courteously and rode on. He had not gone far when he spied a soldier. He rode over.

"Sir, where can I find Governor Lucas?" he asked.

"What's your business with him, boy?"

"That's for Governor Lucas's ears," answered David crisply. And how the soldier stiffened up! thought David. "I report only to him."

The soldier challenged him with his look. David's look was just as bold and as firm as he could make it. Then the soldier wilted and half turned, pointing.

"You see that inn on the corner?"

David nodded.

"Second floor. The Governor's there with the commissioners."

David thanked him and rode on. He dismounted at the inn. He did not feel half as bold as he acted, but he knew he dared not show it. If he slipped once, there was no telling how long it would be before he saw Pa and Ma and the rest of the family again. The little farm in Michigan Territory seemed suddenly very desirable.

He left his horse and walked straight into the inn. He spied the stairs and would have gone right up, had not a militiaman sprung forward to bar his way.

"Hold on, young feller. Where ye aimin' to go?"

David sized him up. He was younger than he looked. His grizzled whiskers might fool people at first glance. David guessed him at thirty.

"I've got a report to make to Governor Lucas."

"Don't recollect ever seein' ye before."

"Don't expect you have," retorted David. "I just slipped out of Toledo ahead of the Michigan militia."

"Did ye now?" The militiaman was perplexed. Can't make up his mind what to do, thought David. "I'd better go up ask the Governor."

"Go right ahead. I'll be behind you."

The militiaman turned and went clumping up the stairs. David followed only a few steps after. His guide went down the oak planking of the second floor hall and knocked on the first door he came to.

"Sergeant McIlwraith, sir."

"Come in."

The sergeant opened the door and stuck his head in. "Beggin' your pardon, sir, but there's a feller here with some kind of word from Toledo."

"Well, send him in. What're you waiting for?"

A little taken aback, the sergeant flung the door open so that David might get by him into the room where the Governor was.

David nodded and grinned at McIlwraith. Then he was in the room.

Governor Lucas sat at a table, around which were three other men. These must be the commissioners Governor Mason had mentioned. Governor Lucas was a man in his fifties, guessed David. His blond hair was whitening except for his eyebrows, which made a straight line across his face under a high, dome-like brow, which was bald of hair. His eyes were small, dark, and piercing. He had a long nose with flared nostrils, and his mouth was a firm, straight line. He was dressed all in black, with a black bow tie at his neck. David thought he looked at him very suspiciously, unless it was his conscience bothering him, for Governor Lucas looked just as upright as Governor Mason, and at least twice as old.

"You're from Toledo, son?" asked the Governor.

"Yes, sir. I set out by dark, so as not to be stopped."

"Your name?"

David saw no reason for lying. It wasn't likely that the Governor of Ohio had ever heard of David Claver or any other Claver related to him. So David told him his name.

"You have some report for us, son? Or are you just in to enlist with us?"

"Sir, I rode down to report that there are twelve hundred militia of the Michigan Territory in possession of Toledo. They're quartered in the houses, and camped about the grounds of the old Fort Industry."

"Half again as many men as our force," said the Governor to the commissioners, who immediately looked very serious.

"Are they all armed?" asked the Governor.

"Sir, they're all armed."

"Any cannon?"

David was in a quandary. He did not know whether there were any cannon. He had not seen any. Still and all, the militia would surely have some larger firing weapons with them.

"I didn't see any," he answered.

"Well, they're no better off than we are," said the Governor.

"But there are so many more of them," observed one of the commissioners.

As far as David could see, Governor Lucas was no more upset by the chance of a battle than Governor Mason. Still, it was clear that neither one entirely discounted the possibility —blood might yet be shed.

"And the people of Toledo?" pressed the Governor. "How do they feel?"

This was a tricky question. He almost said "The people of Toledo," but caught himself in time. Instead, he said, "I guess most of us are for Toledo first, and nothing else matters much unless there's a battle and the town's in danger."

Governor Lucas grinned wryly. "But they've voted in Ohio, just the same." Then he immediately became serious once more. "How did you slip away, Claver? Don't the Michigan militia have sentries posted?"

"Yes, sir. But I got through in the dark before sun-up. Besides, they haven't been there long enough to know all the roads."

"How long?"

"Two days, sir."

The Governor continued to look David over, searchingly, as if he were examining his clothes. It was a lucky thing, David thought, that the militia had never issued any other clothing to him. Or that he had no other signs of the militia about him.

"Do your folks know where you've gone?"

"Yes, sir."

"You'd better not go back. You might be sighted by the Michigan men and taken in."

David did not know what to say. He had not thought about this turn of events. Now he was in trouble. The best thing he could do was to say nothing, in the hope that he would get away somehow. So he just stood there, waiting for Governor Lucas to talk again.

"You can come into our forces and leave us again when we march into Toledo," said the Governor.

"Yes, sir," answered David. There was nothing else he could say.

The Governor got to his feet, strode to the door, jerked it open, and stuck his head out to call, "Sergeant McIlwraith!"

The sergeant came clattering up the stairs as fast as he could. He burst into the room with his gun held ready to fire, looking sort of wild-eyed about him. David almost giggled. The sergeant looked so funny, as if he thought David had overpowered the Governor and the three commissioners and was waiting only for Sergeant McIlwraith to make his appearance to deal with him, too.

"Sergeant, take Mr. David Claver down to General Bell. He wishes to join our militia—at least till we reach Toledo." The Governor turned to David. "My compliments to General Bell. Tell him just what you've told me."

"Yes, sir."

The Governor turned back to the commissioners and began

to talk at once, "As I was saying, we must lose no time re-marking the Harris line . . ."

Then David was beyond the sound of his voice, as he fol-lowed Sergeant McIlwraith back down the stairs. Just the same, he was sharp enough to know that this half-heard sen-tence was the most important information he had received. It would not take Governor Mason long to find out that Governor Lucas had only about eight hundred men against his own twelve hundred; but how could he learn that the Ohio Governor meant to remark the Harris line which would keep the disputed land within the Ohio boundary? David knew he must somehow get away to make his report to Governor Mason.

However, he was in no hurry. Chances were, there was something more to be learned among the Ohio militiamen. So he went docilely along after the sergeant, only half listen-ing to his talk until the other man turned around and chal-lenged him directly.

"Ain't you listenin' to me, Claver? I asked you how many men we'll have to fight—if you know."

"Twelve hundred or so. More'n a thousand, for sure."

"Sure, and you counted 'em!"

"No, I kept my ears open."

"A fine April fool's stunt," mumbled the sergeant to him-self. "Git us all killed. Twelve hundred men! It'll take bullets and bayonets to move 'em!"

David was about to ask where the troops were, but he bit his tongue in time. He was not supposed to know anything about the Ohio militia. Just the same, he was certain they could not be far away, for the sergeant was in no hurry, letting his horse just idle along, going up one street and down another.

"And where'll we get the men?" continued the sergeant. "Ho! the first call for volunteers turned up only half the number asked for—and that was only five hundred. I don't know where we got the eight hundred we've got, and that's a fact!"

"There are more people in Ohio than Michigan Territory," said David.

"Sure, sure—but they ain't got no stomach for fightin'!"

Suddenly they were before the camp of the Ohio militia. The men were encamped about a crude stockade. It was the same kind of stockade the early settlers had built to keep away the Indians, but it looked newer. Perhaps the men had improved on it to spend their time rather than idle it away.

Sergeant McIlwraith passed the sentries, making the way clear for David, and then they rode in among the men. They rode right to the General's quarters and were passed right in.

General Bell was a thin-faced man. David thought his tuft of beard looked as if it had just been pasted on, for it was sparse and straggly. The bushy eyebrows over the keen blue eyes were of a piece with the beard. The General's name was a coincidence; even more, he had some similarity in appearance to Lt. Charlie Bell, too. David guessed they were related.

"With the Governor's compliments, sir," said the sergeant, "but he's sent this man to join up. David Claver."

"Indeed, and are the volunteers following the troops?" the General asked.

"No, sir, this boy's from Toledo."

At this, the General showed some interest. "All right, Sergeant. Go back to your post. Come here, Claver."

David stepped forward.

"Now then, what's the situation in Toledo?"

David told him what he had told Governor Lucas.

General Bell listened with sharp-eyed attention while David spoke. David was uneasily aware of the General's suspicious manner. He suspects me, he told himself, and waited for some kind of trap. It came.

"So the people are of two minds in Toledo, are they?" asked the General bitingly. "How does the Toledo *Gazette* stand?"

As a citizen of Toledo, David would be supposed to know the answer to that question. He didn't. He could only make a guess, good or bad. The paper might not even have declared itself as yet. Chances were, though, that it was on the side of Ohio. David could not afford to hesitate in his answer, either.

"Sir, they're not for Michigan."

"Ah, then they've not changed," said Bell, pleased.

The General was satisfied, too, that David was not a spy. He had been more suspicious than Governor Lucas. Now he began to ask David a series of rapid-fire questions, some of which David answered right away, some of which he could not answer, and said so. Occasionally David thought the General was still testing him. But General Bell had soon exhausted all the information likely to be of interest to the commander of the forces opposing General Brown and the Michigan militia. Done with his questions, he sent an orderly for Lt. Canfield.

The lieutenant came fast, and stood, saluting smartly.

"Lieutenant, we've a recruit for your command. David Claver, late of Toledo."

Lt. Canfield's face brightened. He was a broad-faced young

fellow with the city written all over him. He had a wide mouth which was always ready to grin, showing rather large but even teeth. He could have been about thirty years old, David thought.

"Come along, Claver," said Lt. Canfield.

David followed him from the General's quarters. They went back in among the men. David paused for his horse.

"Got your own horse, I see," said Canfield. "Armed, too?"

"No, Lieutenant."

"Well, we'll issue you a gun when the time comes. We're a little short just now—waiting for the adjutant-general to supply us. Come along and meet the men."

VI.

ESCAPE

I N NO TIME at all, David was making himself at home among
the Ohio men. They were of all ages, very much like those
in the Michigan militia. There was practically no difference
between them. The men in both bodies of troops were young
and old, single and married, and there were even a few ailing
among them.

But now that he was in the Ohio militia, David scarcely
knew what to do. He had remembered the way he had come;
he could find his way out of Perrysburgh easily enough; but
the question now was, when could he get away and back to
Toledo?

In a way, his situation was comical—yesterday in the Michigan militia—today in Ohio's! Still, if the Ohio men had as

much freedom to move around as those in the Michigan
militia, David would not have too much trouble making his
escape when he had the chance.

For a little while David kept to himself. Better not push
himself forward, he thought. But he was not left alone long.
Presently a long-legged fellow with blond hair, as friendly
as a dog, came over and stood next to David.

"My name's Andy Yates," he said. "What's your'n?"
David told him.

"I'm from Cincinnati," Andy went on. "Where you from?"

It was on the tip of David's tongue to mention the farm.
He caught himself. "I came down from Toledo," he said.

"You don't look like a city feller to me," said Andy. "You
reckon this here's gonna be a long fight?"

"Can't tell."

Andy's coming brought over other men. As soon as they
learned that David had come from Toledo, they plied him
with questions. They asked questions as fast as David could
answer them. They were just as anxious to avoid shooting
somebody as the Michigan men were. David told them as
much as they could find out from their own commanders.
But in return, he learned a surprising amount of information
which might be useful to the Governor and the militia of
Michigan Territory.

By such small talk, David found out that the Governor of
Ohio had been busy indeed. He was sending armed citizens
along with the three commissioners who were to remark the
Harris line and re-establish the border. That was to "fool
them Michiganders!" Governor Lucas had also sent down
to President Jackson in Washington to demand that the fed-

eral government send up two commissioners of its own to help settle the border quarrel.

Andy put the feelings of the men when he said, "Ain't nobody here figures to fight. We got it figured out we just been called up to sort of bluff them Michiganders—just like they been called out to bluff us. You figure it'll work?"

"Might be," answered David soberly. "Could be some old coon hunter's apt to slip his finger on the trigger, and then we'd be in it all right."

Andy agreed. "And when them commissioners from Ohio get into that land they're quarrellin' about," he went on, "why like as not, nobody'll bother 'em. They ain't militia. They ain't nobody but ordinary men, and before them Michiganders know it, they'll have that Harris line marked all over again, and we'll be set."

"I'm not so sure about that," said David.

"Well, if the soldiers on their side fire on civilians from ours—why, then the federal government can step right in and put a stop to it," said Andy triumphantly.

"Anyway," put in one of the older men, "we're all set. The minute a shot's fired, the adjutant general's promised to issue a call for three thousand more men! I guess that'll stop the Michiganders!"

"Unless they got more men, too," said David.

"By Gosh! You talk like a Michigander yourself," said Andy.

"No, it's not that," said David quickly. "It's only that I'm trying to think the way they'll think and do."

The older man went on. "Governor Lucas's going to have the legislature make two new counties to cover that land they're fighting about. Then, as soon's he can, they'll show it belongs to Ohio by holding a meeting of the Court of Common Pleas there."

"And when's all that going to happen?" asked David.

"Just as soon as can be. It's April now. The commissioners have to mark the Harris line first."

"And once that's done," concluded Andy, "I reckon them Michiganders will hurry on home and know they're licked."

David said nothing to this. It would be too easy to excite their suspicions if he disagreed. He was sure that he had now learned all he could from the Ohio militiamen. He knew that there were eight hundred men and that they were about as disorganized when it came to arms and ammunition as the Michigan men. The next thing he must do must be to make his way back to Toledo.

As yet, David had no idea how that would be done. He was confident that he would find a way. If he had had a canoe, he could easily float down the Maumee to Toledo, for the river was not far away. He could no longer count on his horse, because it had been put in with other horses in a field next to a row of stables. The horse was just far enough away to make going over after him twice as risky as if David just walked out of camp alone.

David was not worried, except about what Governor Mason might think when he failed to come back as quickly as he should. But he guessed the Governor would bide his time.

It was three days before David made his escape from the Ohio militia.

He had to go on foot, abandoning his horse, which he hated to do. There was no other choice. David had soon learned that the Ohio militia moved around in Perrysburgh just the way the Michigan men did in Toledo. He was wary of taking advantage of this right away. After all, someone might be watching him. If the border dispute were a real war, perhaps then the officers would have been stricter and more cautious. As it was, he soon found out that no one paid him the slightest attention except Andy Yates.

Andy seemed to be always around. Every time David made up his mind to try to escape, Andy was there. He could not tell him to go away. On his third day in camp, David saw Andy coming over.

"Say, the commissioners are set to start for the Harris boundary," he said. "Maybe things'll get moving now."

"That so?" said David, and instantly resolved to stay not another day in camp. But how to make his escape with Andy here?

"Let's walk into town," suggested Andy.

"I'm with you," agreed David.

As he walked along, listening to Andy's chatter, David tried to think of a way he could slip away from him. The more he thought, the more puzzled he got. It was Andy himself who gave him the chance.

"Say, I guess I'll have a drink," he said suddenly, looking toward a tavern. "Comin' along?"

"No thanks," said David quickly. "I don't drink. And I don't much care for taverns. I'll stay outside while you go in, Andy." He was careful not to promise to wait for him, no matter what Andy thought, for he knew that it was now or never. When Andy came out again and failed to find him, he would probably conclude that David had gone back to camp.

The moment Andy vanished into the tavern, David walked

away. He looked for a place to hide until darkness fell. He was handicapped without the horse, but he decided he could make it to Toledo by morning, even by the roundabout route he meant to take.

He could not go by road, for if they determined to look for him, they would naturally search the road and find him in no time at all. When they found him missing, the first thing they'd think of was that he had gone back to Toledo. They might not think he was spying, but only grown home-sick. Many of the younger militiamen talked with longing of the homes they had left behind, and, to tell the truth, David often thought of the little farm west of Detroit with great affection, himself.

He walked to the edge of the village which was farthest away from the camp. Then he went down toward the river. There he was soon lost in a grove of trees. No one had paid any attention to him. He watched carefully from among the trees. There was no sign of pursuit. Had anyone noticed him, it might easily have been thought that he was out to walk back to the camp along the river. Indeed, the camp was within sight of where David hid. Just the same, David was glad he did not have long to wait before sundown and darkness.

There he crouched, where he could see the camp but not be seen himself. The time seemed to drag. But the sun slipped steadily down toward the western rim, and soon it had set.

With the deepening twilight, David struck out along the river's shore for Toledo. He knew the way would be difficult, but with luck he might make as much as two miles an hour, allowing for detours he would have to make on account of the high water.

He was grateful that it was still too early in spring for snakes to be out. No other creature he might startle up in the darkness would be quite as dangerous, even though there could be wildcats and brush wolves. He was hardly out of sight of Perrysburgh before he realized that almost any other course would have been easier. The river shore was often covered by huge trees which had been uprooted by the swift streams of thaw water and carried down until they caught along shore here and there.

Luckily, the sky was clear, and a waxing moon shone high in the southern sky. Once the last daylight had drawn down the west, the moonlight lay palely over everything. Indeed, it seemed quite light. As his eyes grew accustomed to it, David moved quite fast in some places. He knew he would perhaps not have been able to reach his goal without the moonlight to shine along his way.

Two hours after he had started out, David thought he heard sounds of horsemen on the road. Sometimes the hoof-beats sounded close by, sometimes out of sight, as if following the winding of the road along the river. He was sure they might be looking for him, though he had thought the camp so freely run that probably no one except Andy Yates had missed him yet. He did not halt his progress at the sounds from the road. He went as quietly as he could, and only the occasional snapping of a twig marked his progress.

Even so, sometimes he started up animals. Rabbits and foxes darted away; he could not see them, but he knew the sounds they made. Sometimes there were larger animals. David could not be sure what they were, but as long as they moved away from him, he was not worried about them. Now

and then a bird cried out—a blue heron fishing along the river
—a barred owl shouting his "hoo-hoo-hoo-ah!"—a sleepy
sparrow or robin disturbed by his passing.

As the night deepened, he pushed steadily on.

He reached Toledo at dawn.

Tired as he was, David made his way straight to Governor
Mason's quarters. There he was confronted by a sentry who
was not Sergeant McIlwraith.

"Ye can't come in here, boy."

David stopped wearily. "I have to see the Governor. He's
waiting to see me."

The sentry grinned. "Oh, sure—and all the rest of Toledo,
I'm bound!"

"I'm in the militia—I'm not from Toledo," said David.
"What's more, I've been walking all night and I'm dead
tired."

The sentry scratched his head. "What's your proof?"

"I've been on a mission for the Governor and General
Brown. I'm overdue now."

"Well, I ain't had no word to let anybody in. Besides, the
Governor's not up yet."

"I don't expect to wake him. I'll just go in and wait."

"Well . . ." The sentry did not know what to do. He looked
David over carefully, and saw that he was not armed with so
much as a cudgel. Then he shrugged. "I'll tell ye—ye go
inside and sit down where I can see you when I look in now
and then. There's a chair at the foot of the stairs—that'll do
for ye."

He opened the door for David, who slipped quietly in and
sat down. Almost at once he was asleep.

Two hours later, David awoke to the Governor's hand on his shoulder.

"We thought you'd been taken captive," said Governor Mason.

"I was, almost," answered David, rubbing the sleep out of his eyes. "They put me into their militia—I couldn't get away till last night. And then I had to leave the horse."

"No matter. We can find other horses. Now, then, come upstairs. We'll have a little something to eat, and you can tell us what you found out."

General Brown joined them at the breakfast table. The two men listened attentively to all David had to tell. General Brown was pleased to learn that there were fewer Ohioans under arms than Michiganders, and that they were as poorly armed as his own men. Governor Mason could not sit still; he walked up and down across the room, his hands clasped behind his back. Every little while he said. "That's right! That's right! They're playing into our hands."

"How so?" asked General Brown finally.

"Why, if they send commissioners to the Harris line, they'll be violating our territorial laws under the act of last February. It carries a penalty of a thousand dollars fine or five years in jail for anyone except territorial officers who accept office from Ohio or exercise official functions recognized by us in that area. That leaves our hands free—you needn't budge, Joe—just sit tight with your men. The Sheriff of Lenawee County can arrest the commissioners in a civil action. We'll just notify him to make up a posse and wait to hear from us. In the meantime, we'll have to send scouts out to keep track of the commissioners."

Governor Mason turned and cast a doubtful eye at David. "Not him," said the General.

"No, sir," agreed David. "I've seen the commissioners and they've seen me."

"But does anyone else here know them?"

"What difference does that make?" demanded General Brown impatiently. "They'll have quite a party—three men and some kind of armed escort. It won't take this young man to identify anyone. Besides, they'll take their time—mark my words."

"Ten to one, they'll avoid the public roads."

"They'll go around Toledo," agreed the General. "So we'll just have some of the scouts pick them up and report their progress back to us."

"Very well." Governor Mason turned to David and shook hands gravely with him. "We'll meet again, David. Meantime, go back to Lt. Bell's command with our heartiest appreciation."

David was filled with honest pride.

VII.

OFF TO DETROIT

DAVID EXPECTED NO further word from Governor Mason. He had performed the task the Governor had set him, and there was no reason why the Governor should say more to him about what he had done. Yet in ten days, a lantern-jawed orderly from General Brown's staff came to Lt. Bell's unit. He sought out Bell and had David pointed out to him. Then he came over.

"You Claver?" he asked.

"Yes, sir," answered David.

"The Governor wants to see you. Come along. And bring your things."

"You mean everything?"

"All that's yours."

David was mystified. There had been rumors among the militia of some kind of engagement northwest of Toledo. Scouts had brought in word of the progress made by the Ohio commissioners on their way to re-mark the Harris line. Of course, there were all kinds of conflicting rumors. Some militiamen believed that soldiers had gone out to cut off the commissioners, but all the companies were accounted for. Someone had gone, just the same, and though David did not say so, he was quite sure it was someone on the Governor's orders to stand up with the Sheriff of Lenawee County.

But what David thought about the differences between Ohio and Michigan here at what might be the site of a battle did not matter, as he was soon to learn. He was sent up to the Governor's room directly on his arrival at the inn where the Governor was quartered.

This time Governor Mason was alone. He stood with his legs spread wide and his hands clasped together behind him. His eyes were almost merry, though David could see that he was serious enough.

"I told him to tell you to bring your things," he said, without so much as a greeting to David.

"I did, sir. I don't have much. It's all in a knapsack downstairs."

"Good. Now, tell me, David, would you like to leave the militia for a while? They tell me you were brought up in the wilderness. Your people live on one of those farms just hacked out of the woods. Lt. Bell tells me you know tracks and trails as well as a man. To come to the point—I need someone to go into the wilderness."

"I've never been very deep into the wilderness, sir."

"You won't be going alone."

"I wouldn't mind that, either way, if you think I can do it."

"Good. Then it's settled. We leave for Detroit within half an hour."

Their horses were at the door when the Governor signalled David, who had waited patiently. They rode north out of Toledo, returning the way David had come, but keeping along the lake. Detroit was a good day's journey away, but the hour was early, and the Governor did not spare his horse. He was plainly in a hurry. Besides, he was vexed.

For a while, the Governor said nothing. They rode along in silence. The fine April weather was warm and pleasant. Birds were singing on all sides. Killdeers cried out, frightened up as they passed. Mourning doves keened. And song sparrows made their threnodies at every brook and pond. Great flocks of ducks and passenger pigeons went by high over, for the birds were still migrating.

David did not mind the Governor's silence. Riding out into the country made him a little homesick, and he thought of what they would be doing at home now, in this season. They would be turning the earth where the soil could be turned. They would be planting. Ma would be adding to her wild flower garden, and Pa would be teasing her about it, the way he always did.

Governor Mason did not break his moody silence until they stopped for lunch. This had been packed for them by General Brown's staff. It was rough, soldier's fare—salty ham and bread—but David had become accustomed to it. When they sat together in the shade of an old elm tree, the Governor was made to think of the "Toledo war"—as he called it. He began to chuckle.

"Those commissioners you told us about," he began. "We

sighted them. Had men following them all the time. Your friend Nate was one of them. We let them get into Lenawee County. Then the Sheriff's posse went after them. The commissioners got away. They ran like sixty through the cottonwood swamps and left their hats behind. But the Sheriff arrested some of the party. Now they're all claiming our militia fired on them and making a great todo about it all. It'll get them nowhere. We stand pat, and I'd still be there myself if it weren't for this infernal surveyor's report."

Then it came out, and David learned what he was expected to do.

A government surveyor had turned in to Washington a very unfavorable report on the Territory of Michigan.

"The rascal said we'd have five hundred acres of tillable land, and our only possible crops would be swamps, snakes, fever, and the ague!" cried the Governor indignantly.

David had to smile. He knew the report was untrue, but the Governor's anger was amusing because it was plain that Governor Mason was upset enough to want to take his anger out on someone who deserved it, but there was no one for him to vent his anger on.

"It's politics—that's all it is," the Governor went on. "The slave staters don't want Michigan admitted to the Union unless Washington lets Arkansas in, too. They want a slave state for every free state to keep things balanced in Congress. So they send around surveyors to make just the kind of report that'll suit the climate in Washington. We'll reject it. We'll have none of it. We've sent for someone to survey Michigan for us, right and proper, and we'll send in our own survey."

The Governor certainly did not lack fire. His small, stubborn mouth was more set than ever. His face was flushed.

His slender body seemed to vibrate with his angry impatience. At this moment, the Governor looked squarely at David and saw the smile on his lips. For an instant, the Governor's face darkened. His high eyebrows clouded down over his eyes, and David thought that now his anger would be thrown at him. But no, in a moment, Governor Mason's face lightened and he burst out laughing.

"So I'm funny, am I?" he cried. "Well, they'll take account of us down in Washington, mark my words!"

"I'm sure they will," agreed David earnestly.

Nevertheless, he worried a little lest he be unable to fulfill the task the Governor had set for him. He did not understand clearly as yet what he must do, except to go with the surveyor and help him, though he knew nothing much about surveying, apart from the measurements they had made on the farm. And how little that was! But he could learn.

"It's always a good thing to have a sense of humor, David," resumed the Governor. "I could hardly stand myself if I lacked it. It's as important as gumption—and I reckon you've got plenty of that. It was a bold, brave thing you did to go down into the Ohio camp. More than anything else, that's responsible for your being here. When I had word that the surveyor was in Detroit and ready to set out, I knew he'd want somebody who had enough flint in him to do him in good stead. I thought of you right away. Besides, we need somebody who can keep still about this business till we're ready for those fellows in Washington."

"Thank you, sir."

"Don't go thanking me. Thank your parents and the Providence that made you what you are. It's good training does it, boy!"

It was early evening when they reached Detroit.

Detroit was the largest settlement at the western end of the lake route from the eastern part of the United States. David had been in the city once before, when he had come through with his family from Vermont. He knew Detroit lay on the west bank of a small lake named St. Clair, and beside the Detroit River, which connected that lake to Lake Erie. But even though he had been there only a few years before, the city had changed so much in that short time that he hardly recognized it. Besides, that first time he had come in from the water side of Detroit, and the city looked altogether different from the land side.

Here there were rough houses, together with Indian encampments. A few Indians came to barter and trade. They set up crude camps on the edge of the settlement, until they had got what they had come to get. This was usually firewater, which they were forbidden to have. The houses were set in uneven rows. These rows, in turn, were divided, farther on into the city, by roads much worse than David had traveled. The roads were not only pitted and rutted, but overrun with pigs and geese.

David did not know how many people lived in Detroit. He knew only that there had been a few thousand when he had first gone through the city. Now there were many more. Detroit was sprawled out in every direction, but the Governor knew just which way to go. He pushed toward the center of the settlement, where a few taller buildings rose.

"You've been here before, David?" asked Governor Mason, turning in his saddle.

"Only when we went through a few years ago, sir."

"It's grown since then. A thousand people a day pass

through here for the western part of the Territory when ships can make the lakes. That rascally surveyor!"

They went on. The rough log cabins on the outskirts gave way to occasional frame houses, and even now and then to buildings made of bricks. But most of the buildings in this port of Detroit were one-time log houses to which frame ells and lean-tos had been added, as families grew and prospered.

Soon they came within sight of the lake, though David smelled the freshness of the water before he saw much of it. They were now in the oldest part of Detroit. There some of the older buildings had been torn away to make room for two and three storey buildings.

Governor Mason reined up in the middle of a crossroad. He paid no attention to the movement of people and other horsemen around him. He turned to David.

"David, I want you to go to my house. It's down that street half a mile or so. Look for a hitching-post shaped like a horse's head, painted white. It stands in front of the house. Here,"—he paused to take from his pocket a note he had written before he left Toledo—"give the housekeeper this message from me. And wait there till I come."

The Governor wheeled away almost before David could acknowledge his instructions.

David turned down the street in the direction Governor Mason had given. So quickly was the day now drawing to its close, with the appearance of clouds in the west, that David knew he would have to hurry if he were to have light enough even to see a white hitching post. There were no street lights. If one wished to travel in the city, it must be by lanternlight. He hurried down the street, looking sharply to right and left.

Half a mile, the Governor had said. When he judged he

had gone that far, David watched more sharply than ever. But he saw the white hitching post in the shape of a horse's head from some distance. Soon he stood before the door of the house, knocking.

He waited for what seemed a long time. He knocked twice more. He was beginning to think he had come in vain when he heard steps approaching inside. Then the door was pulled cautiously open and an oil lamp was thrust out at him, held aloft in the hand of a middle-aged woman.

"What is it?" she asked, opening the door wide now that she saw it was just a boy who stood there.

"If you please, Ma'am, Mr. Mason sent me."

"Mr. Mason's not home," said the woman, starting to close the door.

"I have a letter from him."

The door stopped moving, held uncertainly where it was. The woman did not know what to do, but she could hardly refuse a letter from Governor Mason.

"He's in town," David went on. "I rode to town with him."

"Give me the letter, then."

David did so. She began to close the door again, but this time she thought better of it. She opened the door wide and stepped out of the way.

"It's a letter from him, right enough," she said, having looked at the handwriting. "So ye must have seen him. Lord! I never know where he is from one day to the next."

"We came in from Toledo," explained David.

Behind him, the woman closed and locked the door.

As she passed him, she looked at him once more with narrowed eyes. "Ain't had overmuch to eat, either, have ye?"

she asked. Without waiting for his reply, she added, "Come along. Ye can eat with me, if ye can stand the common food."

"Thank you, Ma'am."

David followed her into the rear of the house. Food was on the kitchen table. The woman had been at a frugal meal when his knock had interrupted her. A thick potato soup, some slices of ham, a dark, coarse bread, and what seemed to be tea. Just looking at it made David hungry at once, for the soldiers' fare he and Governor Mason had eaten on the way had not satisfied his hunger.

"Likely ye've got a name, boy," said the woman.

"David Claver, Ma'am."

"Well, Davie, here's a plate. Set to, and welcome."

She did not offer him her own name. David did not trouble himself about it. He began to eat heartily, while the woman opened the letter David had brought. She read the few lines hastily scribbled there. Then she looked up and examined him all over again.

"Been at the front, have ye?" she asked. "Never'd a thought they taken boys."

"Mostly not boys," he explained.

"And ye're to stay here till he comes. Lord knows when that'll be! He's as like as not to go rushing off to some other part of the Territory!"

David did not think her fears were justified. Just the same, he was made a little uneasy at the thought that Governor Mason might forget that he was here and leave him sitting.

She began to ply him with questions. She wanted to know where he had got into the militia, where he had come from, where his family was. She asked so many questions, David understood, because she was alone for long periods at a time, and did not have enough people to talk to. He answered as well as he was able to. Finally she was satisfied. Then she began to think of what was to be done with him until the Governor came.

"Since there's no telling when he'll be here," she said, "ye might as well rest in his study. Come."

She got up, took the lamp again, and led David part way back along the hall down which he had come. She turned off into a high-ceilinged room filled with books. She pointed to a low couch against the farther wall.

"Ye can sleep there, boy. If ye get cold—and it'll be cold here before long—cover yerself with that buffalo robe."

Hardly giving him time to reach the couch, the woman withdrew. With her went the lamp and all the light.

David took off his shoes, lay down, and pulled the buffalo robe up around him. The couch was hard, but he was so tired that any bed would have seemed soft to him. That he was in a strange room and a strange house did not bother him at all. He knew he was closer to home than he had been for some time. He wondered how long he would have to wait for Governor Mason to come. And he thought proudly that here he was resting in the Governor's own home, and only the night before he had been in camp.

But he was too tired to lie thinking long. Soon he was fast asleep.

VIII.

A VISIT HOME

IT WAS ALMOST midnight when David was awakened by a hand shaking him by the shoulder, coupled with the soft calling of his name. He sat up.

Governor Mason was at his side. Another man was bent over the desk, studying something by the light of a lamp.

The Governor saw that David was awake and said, "Come over and meet Mr. Suydam, David."

David swung his feet off the couch.

Richard Suydam was the surveyor for whom Governor Mason had sent. He had come by boat. He was a tall, hungry-looking man, with curly black hair and snapping dark eyes. He wore a little pointed beard, as black as his eyes, and he had a high color in his cheeks. He had a mischievous look about him. His smile made David feel he had known him a long time.

"Well, David, you're a sturdy young fellow," said Suydam. "Mr. Mason promised me that. I could have used two of you."

"Oh, we can find someone else, Suydam," said the Governor.

"I wanted to leave in the morning."

"By that time, then."

"Man, it's past midnight!"

David had an inspiration. "Sir," he said to Governor Mason, "if I may speak . . ."

"Go right ahead."

"Well, sir, there's Nate. Nate Pendleton. It's true, he's in the militia at Toledo, but couldn't he be sent for? He could meet us wherever Mr. Suydam says."

"We ought to be able to find someone here in Detroit."

The surveyor interrupted. "A special friend of David's?" he asked thoughtfully. "Perhaps they'd work better as a pair. Does he know the country?"

David's heart sank. Of course, Nate did not know the country—not nearly as well as David, and David counted his knowledge of the Territory away from the neighborhood of home as hardly anything at all.

"No better than I, sir," David answered truthfully.

"After all, it's *your* job to know the country," said the Governor to the surveyor. "And to tell those politicians in Washington what it's really like."

Suydam grinned. "Where do you think he could meet us?" he asked David.

Once again David could only tell the truth. "Sir, Nate

wouldn't know enough of the country to meet us except where
he's been. We might be able to get to Saginaw Bay in two
—three days, but Nate might not. I thought, sir, as long as
we're this near, we could start into the Territory by way of
my Pa's farm. We might stop there till Nate could catch up
with us. He's been that way. He could make it in less time
than it would take him to come to Detroit and then follow us."

Governor Mason shrugged. "He can be sent for—if you
want him."

Suydam stood for a moment undecided, his black eyes fixed
without moving on David. Then he spoke, with a casual toss
of his head. "I'm used to wilderness travel. Let him come."

"You won't gain anything going by way of the farm," said
the Governor.

"Yes, I will," replied Suydam. "The boy's been away from
home just long enough to want to see his folks. I can't blame
him. He'll be the better for it." He turned to David and
added, "Now get some sleep, lad. We'll be off in the morning,
and trust to the Governor to send a courier to Nate at once."

"Very well," agreed Mason. "Just so one thing's understood—I want the survey made as fast as possible—before
those politicians in Washington forget that Michigan Territory exists."

Suydam looked at David and nodded confidently.

In the morning they ate a huge breakfast prepared by Governor Mason's housekeeper. Because the Governor was there,
the woman was silent, though David could see she ached to
ask as many questions of the surveyor as she had asked him
the previous night.

The Governor did all the talking. He filled their ears with

instructions. More than once David caught a hint of a smile on Suydam's lips. The surveyor seemed to know as well as David that Mason was more enthusiastic than practical. Half the things the Governor expected them to do would not or could not be done in the short time he expected them to be gone.

Governor Mason saw them off. "Nate Pendleton will have my message by noon today at the latest," he promised David. "If he sets out right away, he should be at your father's farm tomorrow."

David and Suydam made quite a procession on their way out of Detroit. Each rode a strong horse, and each trailed another horse. One horse was meant for Nate. The other was a pack horse, laden with all kinds of supplies. They could not expect to carry enough food for the entire trip. They would have to depend on hunting, fishing, and food supplied by Indians along the way. Each of their own horses carried saddlebags, too, and the surveyor's carried the tools of his profession.

Most of the time, Suydam was silent as they rode along. Now and then they paused, and at such times Suydam asked David all kinds of questions. He asked about David's family, how long he had lived in the Territory, and how he liked Michigan.

At the same time, he volunteered a little information about himself. He was fifteen years older than David. He had been a surveyor for as many years. He was married and had a son half David's age back in Vermont. Soon David felt that he knew him as well as Suydam wanted him to.

It was strange, when the surveyor asked David what he wanted to do, David could not answer, except to say he

thought he would like to do anything but farm. Yet each
time David said he didn't think he'd like to do what his
father did, Suydam would say, "It takes a strong man to
live close to the land. And a good one!"

David did not know what to reply. He had already learned
that a soldier's life was not all excitement. It had just as many
long hours in it as a farmer's life. Suydam's attitude puzzled
David. It seemed to him just as if Suydam were all in favor
of a farmer's life.

Late in the day, they reached the farm.

Willie, who was at work in one of the fields, saw them
first. He did not recognize David right away. But, after a
long stare, he knew his brother was one of the two riders.
He dropped his hoe among the rows of potatoes and came
running down to the rail fence which had been put up along
the road since David had left.

"Hey, Davie!" he cried. "Is the war over?"

"I don't know. I'm not in the militia any more," David
answered. "How's everybody?"

"Fine! We miss you, though. Specially me."

David laughed. He explained to Suydam that his brother
meant that, since David was gone, he had had to shoulder all
David's farm work. He introduced Willie to the surveyor.

When they started forward again, Willie took a short cut
angling off through the fields. He ran, calling the house. By
the time David and Suydam rode into the yard, Ma, Ginny
and even Baby Joey were standing expectantly in the doorway. But not Pa. So David knew Pa was at work in some
other corner of the farm—probably in the north ten.

Soon they were all sitting around the kitchen table, and
David was explaining his new mission. He was surprised at

how good it felt to be in this familiar room once more, to be able to look out of the window and see the land that was their own. He had never thought it would be like this when he had set out less than two months ago.

Soon Pa was there, too. His keen eyes searched his son's face for any sign of change. He acknowledged his introduction to Mr. Suydam very soberly.

"Ye've not come home then," he said to David. "Not tired of war?"

"No, Pa. I'm to travel with Mr. Suydam. It's the Governor's wish."

Pa did not say anything, but David could see he didn't like it. David knew Pa expected him back to help with the work. He explained to them all that they had come here to wait for Nate. It was perhaps the only chance he would have to see his family for many weeks.

"We're glad you came, Davey," said Ma.

"And we'll be gladder still when ye've come to stay," added Pa.

David grinned. Pa would never change.

"And what is it now ye're after in the wild woods?" asked Pa.

David did his best to answer. "The Governor wants a new survey made, Pa. The old survey was made by a man who said there wasn't as much as five hundred acres that would grow crops in all Michigan Territory east of Lake Michigan,"

"Why, that's a lie!" cried Pa, shocked.

David nodded. "The Governor's pushing for this part of the Territory to become a separate State. Down in Washington they're putting him off. South of us Ohio and the Territory are quarrelling about a strip of land each one claims.

So the Governor wants to know all we can find out about the Territory to take it to Washington and lay it before them down there."

"He wants something to bargain with," guessed Pa.

"I guess that's it," agreed David.

Now it was his turn. He plied Pa with questions. How much more land would he clear? How many more fields would he turn? And who would take a hand with the work when Willie, too, was gone?

"I ain't goin'," said Willie promptly.

"Maybe you've got more sense than I have," said David, smiling.

Even as he said it, David thought sincerely that in a way he meant it. Once the excitement of being among the soldiers had worn off, David had realized soon enough that being a militiaman was no more important than being a farmer, except that you saw a little more of the world. And maybe that wasn't all it was talked up to be!

Everything here wore the face of dear familiarity. David was tied to it by a thousand cords of memory which reached back through his childhood. He was filled with a warm glowing at the way in which Joey's scrubbed pink face turned toward him—at the shine in Ginny's eyes—at Willie's only half-suppressed envy—at Ma's unashamed delight at seeing her eldest son again.

That night David told of his adventures in the militia. Mr. Suydam had wisely chosen to go to bed, for he had had very little sleep the night before and wanted to be fresh for the journey.

As David sat at the fireplace with his brothers and his sister, he felt that he had never had such a sense of belonging among them. It wasn't that the adventure of going into the outside world no longer beckoned him. It was only that here he was among his own people. It was strange how just a little while away from home had changed his mind a little about the farm in the wilderness of the Michigan Territory.

And how all their faces lit up as he talked. It was like telling them a story. Pa and Ma listened to every word, too. Ma sat rocking gently, smiling, and Pa sat with a faraway look in his eyes. Maybe he, too, had once wanted to go out into the world! And the warmth that held them was more than that which came from the fire on the hearth.

Nate Pendleton came early next morning.

David, who had slept before the hearth, heard the approach of horses outside. The horses meant for the journey had whinnied and stirred around as the strange horses came up from the west. It was scarcely dawn. David got up and ran to look out.

Nate was just getting off his horse. There was another horse, too. On it rode a stranger to David.

David got into his trousers and shirt and hurried outside.

Nate was busy tying the horse he had ridden to the saddle of one of the other horses belonging to Mr. Suydam. Just as David came running out, the other rider started forward toward Detroit. So he must be the Governor's messenger, thought David.

"Well, Dave you're a welcome sight to see," Nate greeted him.

"So're you. Mr. Suydam's not up yet, but he'll be glad you're here already."

"Now, hold on! Who's Mr. Suydam? What's all this about?" asked Nate.

David explained as they walked to the house.

By this time Pa and Ma were up, too. Ma was already getting breakfast. David introduced Nate to his parents.

"Just sit down," said Ma. "Breakfast'll be right on."

"We'd better wait for Mr. Suydam," said David.

"He's stirring. He'll be here," said Pa. He turned to Nate. "How's the war?"

"I wouldn't call it a war," Nate answered, with a twinkle in his eye. "More like two armies making faces at each other, and that's a fact. The Michiganders have taken over Toledo. The Toledo *Gazette* scolds Michigan. General Brown hollers he'll burn out the *Gazette* because it's all for Ohio. The Ohioans say they'll come up and wipe us all out."

"Oh, I hope not," cried Ma.

"Don't you worry none, Ma'am," said Nate hastily. "All the runnin' they've been doin' has been down into Ohio— not this way. It's all just a lot of loud talk on both sides. Oh, they rode one or two fellers on rails and such like—but if anybody's got shot, I ain't heard about it." He grinned. "It ain't much like soldiering, and that's a fact. I was mighty glad when I found out I was to come back here—even if I didn't know what it was for."

Just then the surveyor came in.

While David introduced him to Nate, Suydam stood taking Nate's measure the way he had taken David's.

"You'll make a good pair," he said at last. "I could wish you knew a little more about the wilderness . . ."

"More?" interrupted Nate. "I don't know anything."

"You'll learn. And fast, too. Did you ride all night?"

"Most of it, yes, sir," answered Nate. "But I'm not tired. About all we've been doing down there at Toledo is sleep. So I've had my fill of that."

"Ready to go, then. Good."

"Yes, sir."

"We'll leave right after breakfast," continued Suydam. "We'll not go west at this point, because that's the Chicago turnpike. That's well enough known. We'll travel north. We'll keep to the Indian trails as much as we can, and try to get over some of the Territory this side of the lake. We may even cross to the other side—though I know Governor Mason's not interested in that part of the Territory."

There were few preparations to be made for the journey. Suydam had not unpacked anything because he had decided Nate would be here in time to start with them.

But for David there were once again all the farewells to be made. And this time he lingered a little, standing with Pa and Ma and the others even after the surveyor and Nate were mounted. The last thing Pa said to him was, "Any time ye figure to come back here, son—there's a place for ye."

IX.

INTO THE WILDERNESS

Not far east of the Claver home, a trail led northward. When they came to it, David turned north.

The surveyor called a halt.

David swung his horse around to face Suydam, and Nate came from behind.

"What's up, Mr. Suydam?" David asked.

"I want to be sure where we're going."

"North, sir. You said to go north."

"That's right, David. Where does this road lead?"

"The next place on it is Mr. Brighton's. Then comes Mr. Howell's. After that, I don't know."

"The Governor says we're not to waste time on the southern counties of the Territory. They're already well settled, and those west of Detroit are well enough surveyed. We're to go to Saginaw and push north. Will this trail get us to Saginaw?"

David hesitated. He did not know.

Nate spoke instead. "The Saginaw road leads up from Detroit, Mr. Suydam. I reckon if we push on this way we'll find some trail that leads across to the settlement of Flint. The Saginaw road lies through that place."

"You've been there, Nate?"

"No, sir. My uncle has though."

The surveyor drew a crudely drawn map from his pocket. He pored over this for a little while. David and Nate looked at it, too. They saw that it was a rough map of the Michigan Territory. Detroit and Dearborn were marked on it. So were Flint and Saginaw, and, far up, an island named Mackinac. The road to Saginaw was marked, too. So were the Chicago turnpike, the Territorial Road, and the Grand River Trail southwest. The trail they were on was not marked. David could see that the map had been hastily drawn. He guessed that the Governor had made it for the surveyor.

"Very well," said Suydam, folding the map. "Go on, David."

The trail to the north was wide enough to permit passage of wagons. It had begun as an old Indian trail, but the first settlers had widened it so that they could bring their household goods through. This was not as much work as a newcomer might have expected because the trail led through many open places. There tall grass waved. Even now, in spring, the grass was almost a foot high. In summer it would be as much as five feet in many places.

There was not much underbrush. The Indians who had

lived here before the settlers came had always set fire to the underbrush and burned it away. Therefore the woods were easy to travel through. The trail led through open prairie, sometimes through woods, and sometimes through oak groves which stood surrounded by openings which were already bright green with new grass, starred here and there with flowers. Now and then they came to open places blue with violets.

They were two hours on the trail before they met a fellow-traveler. David recognized him at once when he caught sight of the horseman coming toward them.

"It's the Reverend Sommers—the traveling preacher," he said to Suydam.

As the preacher came near, David hailed him.

"Why, it's David Claver!" exclaimed the traveler. His pale blue eyes lit up with pleasure, and his lips broke into a smile. "Weren't you down south in the militia?"

"Yes, sir, I was. But I'm here now."

David explained and introduced his companions.

"I've just come from Howell's place—there's two, three places all around there now," said the Reverend Sommers. "They're thinking of making a town of it."

They talked for a short time. David remembered warmly how often the preacher had spent the night at the Claver house on his way to Detroit. That would be where the Reverend Sommers was going now.

"You're familiar with this Territory, Reverend Sommers?" asked Suydam.

"Tolerably."

"We hope to reach Saginaw," continued Suydam.

"You'll find a cross-trail above Howell's place."

"That's what we need to know. Thank you, sir."

Before going on, the preacher had a few words for David. "I could see last time I visited your home your father was none too pleased at your going off. But I knew it was in you to go. I saw it coming. There comes a time a lad must show he's soon to be a man, and there's no stopping him. But, Lad, remember this—a man who goes with God in his heart and his own land under his feet—provided he has sense enough to appreciate what is his—that man has the greatest treasure life can give."

Then they parted. David saw the preacher going off toward the Claver farm with the secret wish to be there to greet him when he arrived. But his way led north, not south.

It was not long before they reached the Brighton farm. Here stood three houses, all grouped together, as if for comfort in this wild land. They were of logs. One had a rail fence to set it off from the woods on the one side and the trail on the other. That, said David, was Mr. Brighton's place. He had been the first to settle there.

They waved at women and children who were outside, but they did not stop. David would have liked to visit, since he knew the Brighton family, but Suydam said gently that they could not afford to take time to do so. It was already in the middle of the morning, and if they did not hurry, night would find them somewhere on the trail.

"We'll have many a night to spend under the stars," said Suydam. "We won't have to start now if we can reach Flint by nightfall."

They passed Howell's settlement later, again without stopping.

Not far north of it, just as the preacher had told them,

a trail crossed east to west. Here they paused briefly to eat lunch. But Suydam hardly gave them time to eat before he was urging them to be off again.

They turned east. This trail was not made for wagons. It was still only an Indian path, made for a solitary traveler on foot or horse. They could not travel as fast here as they could earlier in the day.

They had not gone far before they came to a river.

"Look for the fording place," said Suydam. "We'll have to get used to crossing rivers."

They had only to follow the path, for it led along the shore to a shallow place in the water. David urged his horse forward without fear. He was a little alarmed as water mounted higher and higher along the horse's legs, but even in mid-stream it did not reach higher than the horse's belly.

Soon they were on the west bank of the river, pushing on toward their goal.

At sundown they came to the settlement of Flint City. In the light of the setting sun, the scattered buildings seemed to glow as with gold. David and Nate were happy to see the settlement. After traveling all afternoon without seeing anyone, they could now look forward to a restful night, promised Nate, in Jake Smith's tavern and hostelry.

"My uncle stopped here. Jake runs the ferry, too," Nate said.

Flint City was only a little larger than Howell's place. Here there were more buildings, and the road looked more like a street. Nate knew about the town because his uncle had told him. It was older than any of the farms in that part of the Territory where David lived, but not much. Everything in this Michigan Territory except Detroit and Mackinac and some of the places along the Chicago turnpike was new.

The buildings were mostly of logs. The tavern was of logs and clapboard. But it was no longer Jake Smith's, as Nate had said. Like so many pioneers, Jake had gone. Nate learned when Suydam talked with the proprietor that Jake had only owned the land, and that the present proprietor had built the tavern and started the ferry.

Nor did the settlement offer either comfortable sleeping or a restful night. People seemed to be traveling in numbers between Saginaw and Detroit and sleeping room was limited. The three of them had to sleep at close quarters on the floor in a room just off the bar-room. Noise from the bar kept them awake half the night. And from outside every now and then came the sounds of the ferry, loading or unloading passengers. Once there was a fight just outside; loud voices and hard blows woke David after midnight.

Suydam got the boys up at dawn. Since they had slept in their clothes, they were ready to start traveling at once. Suydam, however, preferred to buy breakfast at the tavern, and their supplies for the wilderness north of Saginaw.

The proprietor's wife, a heavy woman in middle age, waited on them. She took a motherly interest in David and Nate. She smiled at them constantly, and she seemed to think they could not get enough to eat.

"And where you off to?" she asked finally.

"Way up north," said David.

Her eyes widened. "Why, they do say there's not a soul living on the other side of Saginaw all the way to the Pacific Ocean!" she cried. "The Indians'll get you."

Suydam grinned and winked at David.

The proprietor added, "Siberia, they call it—the Siberia of Michigan. Nought but Indians and animals can live there."

A frown furrowed Nate's forehead. A glance at the surveyor reassured David. Suydam's eyes were twinkling.

"West is the way the pioneers are going," said Suydam. "We aim to be first in some places."

The kind-hearted woman insisted on packing a lunch for them. She appeared to be distressed because they were going to Indian country. She acted as if she would never lay eyes on them again.

"It's people like that who give the Territory a bad name," said Suydam, as they left the tavern. "No wonder Washington has so poor an opinion of the proposed State!"

The ferry was a crude affair. It was only a large barge, partly poled across, partly drawn by horses, two teams of which served on each shore of the broad river. The ferryman was talkative. Once they were safely aboard and cast off, he warned them that the good road ended only a few miles from Flint. He called Flint "Grand Traverse," because that had been the original name of the settlement.

"The soldiers—they fixed the road all the way from Detroit," he told them. "Been at it since I can remember—before the ferry was here—but I reckon they got tired. Anyways, you can get through to Saginaw—but I wouldn't try to git a wagon up that way."

The ferry moved slowly but steadily, despite the pull of the current. Soon they were on the far side. The road there seemed as broad as it had been coming into Flint City. There were even a few ground-hugging log cabins on this side of the river.

But soon the road began to narrow. They were little more

than an hour beyond Flint. At the same time, it became more uneven. Finally it became only a trail, sometimes single, sometimes a crude double path.

The further they got from Flint, the more the character of the country changed. At first it was scarcely to be noticed. But gradually David realized that there were fewer oak openings. They encountered more swamps which made travel more difficult, for they had to pick their way with care.

Then, too, the country grew less even. There were fewer flat areas. The farther north they got, the more rolling the country seemed. Little knolls grew into gentle hills. These gave way to high hills and bluffs. This rolling country was often covered with forests of pine and hardwood trees. The forests seemed to grow thicker as they went on.

David was keenly aware of the contrast between this kind of woodland and that at home. West of Detroit the woods seemed to be mostly of smaller trees, but here the trees towered high. The woods at home were light with the sun's glow, but these woods were dark even at noon. And in the pine woods especially there seemed always to be a waiting presence in the pungent twilight.

The way they traveled was not as lonely as the east-west trail had been the day before. Though it was not crowded, the road was not theirs alone. They passed a fur-trader on his way to Flint. After him came two Indians of the Huron nation. Like all Indians, they wanted to trade something. Suydam gave them a little tobacco, which satisfied them.

In the middle of a pine forest, they came upon a family moving south by wagon. A man, a woman, and two young boys. The wagon was drawn by a team of horses, and two cows were tied to the tail of the wagon. The three travelers from the south came just in time to lend a hand with the repair of a wheel which had come off the heavily laden wagon.

"Ain't no country fit for man or beast," the man complained. "I'm headin' fer the Chicago turnpike."

"He's a movin' man," said the woman wearily.

"Whar ye bound fer?" asked the man.

Suydam gestured north.

"Everybody to his own taste, I guess," he answered. "Me, I like it whar it's a mite more restful, and thar ain't so much land to be cleared." He nodded knowingly. "Ye won't stay up thar long, mind my words!"

They parted. The wagon jogged off to the south, facing trail too narrow for it. Suydam looked after them.

"Sounds dreary, eh, boys?" he asked. "Just the same, some folks are staying."

They set out again.

This day there was no pause for lunch. They ate as they rode, and stopped only to feed and water the horses. There was never any shortage of water. The trail skirted little ponds and crossed creeks and small rivers. The late spring day grew warm enough to make them grateful for the coolness of the pine forests.

Though they pressed steadily on, there was no sign of a settlement. Not so much as a log hut broke the wilderness. And as the day drew to a close, there were no longer travelers to be met.

The sun went down, and soft dusk came to the trail. Still they went on, as twilight deepened, and a great saffron afterglow spread across the western sky. A waxing moon shone out of the southwest, riding the pale green edge of the afterglow. Out of the dark, the whippoorwills began to call.

Anxious as he was to reach Saginaw, Suydam drew rein at the edge of a river which they reached in the deepening darkness.

"I'm afraid there's no help for it, boys," he said. "We'll sleep here tonight. We can't hope to ford a strange river by night."

They found a soft bank under a pine tree and prepared for the night. Nate wanted to build a bonfire and had already begun to gather twigs when Suydam stopped him.

"One of the first rules to learn about traveling in unknown country is never to draw attention to yourself," he said. "If hostile Indians are nearby, a campfire could be seen for miles."

They dipped into their supplies for supper and sat by the wan light of the moon, talking over the events of the day.

"You're not sorry you came along?" Suydam asked, just before they slept.

"No, sir!" chorused David and Nate.

"All right. Go to sleep. We'll get an early start again."

In the morning they discovered only a short distance beyond the river where they had spent the night, a cluster of buildings—a sawmill, a church, the abandoned garrison building, a store, a tavern, and twenty log cabins—which were Saginaw City.

X.

UNKNOWN COUNTRY

Though the country north and west of Saginaw was unsettled by white men, trails led through it. In less than an hour after their arrival at Saginaw, they were on one of them. They had stopped in Saginaw to buy lunch to carry with them. And Suydam had asked some of the Saginaw settlers, particularly one old trapper, what the country was like to the north.

They had not learned much.

"Ain't a white man up thar," said the trapper. "Indians a-plenty. Mostly friendly. Ain't many trails, either—but sometimes they're purty good. Most of 'em lead to Indian villages. Plenty of animals for food. Ye won't starve."

The trail they followed led for many miles northwestward

along a river. It was hard to follow, for it was not as clearly marked as trails south of Saginaw. The forest crowded down to the river's edge. Indeed, the trees away from the trail were so dense that passage among them was almost impossible except for a man on foot.

Nor were there in these woods the birds with their chatter commonly heard in more open places. The forest was of pine, maple, beech, and ash trees, and such nut-bearing trees as walnut and butternut. Cherry trees were bunched along the edge of the woods, and far back from the river great poplars stood out. Here, unlike the country to the south, the forest floor was often covered with blackberry growth, hazel bushes, and wild grape vines.

Now and then there were still oak openings. It was past mid-day when they came to the first of them. Instead of riding across the grassy expanse before them, Suydam stopped and dismounted.

"This is where our work begins," he said.

David and Nate got off their horses and let them graze. They helped Suydam get his tools from the pack-horse. David knew something about surveying, and it was plain to him that Suydam was more than a surveyor.

"You didn't think the Governor wanted only measurements, did you?" answered Suydam when David asked. "I'm a geologist, too. I study the ground and look for minerals. We've been sent out to make a list of assets for the Governor to take or send to Washington."

Suydam did very little surveying. Instead, he dug deep down into the ground in various places—in the middle of the oak groves, in the open prairie, in the deep forest. He examined the ground. In some places the soil was a gravelly loam that went down well over a foot. In others, it was more than three feet of clay. In still others it was as many feet of rich loam. And in the woods the soil lay under a foot-deep mulch of leaves.

"It's no wonder the grass grows so high or the woods stand so full," said Suydam. "I've seldom seen soil so rich. The Governor will be pleased to learn of it."

He made many notes in a book he carried with him. He put down such things as the nature of the soil, and what grew on it, even to the names of flowers now in bloom—lilies-of-the-valley, violets, bellwort, and the first wild roses. He also wrote down the names of all the different kinds of birds they saw or heard, including the owls and whippoorwills which called all night long.

When they went forward again, it was only to stop at another place for the same purpose. Now and then, the three of them rode off in several directions from the trail to find brooks and lakes so clear that the bottom could be seen from the surface six feet above.

Sometimes Suydam waded into a lake to scoop up the pebbles of its bottom and examine them.

Because of this study of the land, they did not make much distance.

"We'll just have to get used to this," said Suydam as they camped that night under a canopy of oak trees.

"How many miles do you figure we made?" asked Nate.

"Not more than twenty, if that much," answered Suydam.

As they sat in the darkness by the light of the waxing moon, they talked of how long it would take them to reach the upper tip of Michigan Territory. David guessed as much as two weeks. Nate was more pessimistic; he thought it would take at least a month. Suydam himself estimated twenty days.

"I'd guess we've got about two hundred miles to go from Saginaw—maybe more," said Suydam. "We'll have to make some detours, I expect—around lakes and swamps. We can't hope to go in a straight line."

"And we'll likely run into deeper woods," said Nate.

David made no guess. He knew little about this northern part of the Territory. Besides, every evening his thoughts turned back toward home, and he wondered what they were all doing there now. Eating supper, doing chores, sitting around the fireplace. Did they think of him too? he wondered.

On their fourth day from Saginaw, just as David was preparing to cross a shallow brook through which the trail led, he saw a fresh footprint in the wet sand of the water's edge. He pulled up his horse, dismounted, and knelt to look at it.

Behind him, Suydam got down from his horse and came up.

David pointed to the footprint. "That's an Indian footprint, Mr. Suydam."

"Fresh, too."

"Yes, sir. Look at the way the water's oozing into it. He was here only a few steps ahead of us."

"Didn't hear a thing," said Nate.

"No, and you won't," answered David.

"We'll have to get out our guns," said Nate.

"That would be the worst thing you could do," replied David. "They're probably watching us right now. If they'd wanted to kill us, they could have done it already, easy."

"You seem to know a good deal about Indians, David," said Suydam.

"Yes, sir. You can't farm in Indian country without getting

to know something about them. Many a time they came to the farm—especially the first year we were there—and we never saw them come. They were just there, all of a sudden. Not so much as a leaf stirred when they came. They can move like shadows."

"What do we do?" asked Nate.

"We go on," said Suydam.

They remounted and pushed across the stream.

David, in the lead, was very conscious of eyes upon him. Yet he could see nothing. He knew, just the same, that Indian scouts had probably seen them some way back, and had been watching them ever since. The path they followed in this place showed signs of being more used. It was beaten down and wider, though there were few signs of horses having traveled here. Few of the Indians had horses, as much as he knew. At least, all the Indians who had ever presented themselves at the Claver house had come on foot.

David was sure they must be nearing an Indian village. He said as much over his shoulder to the surveyor. He pointed to the signs in the well-used trail at this place.

In less than half an hour, they reached the shore of another river. There, across the water on the opposite shore was a Chippewa Indian village. It was not a large one. It was made up of scarcely a dozen lodges. These were long and low buildings, put together with stones and bark. Some were round, like wigwams. All were arranged around an open place, from which the smoke of a fire rose above the village.

The Indians themselves were crowded down to the edge of the water. They had plainly been expecting them. Not a sound came from the Chippewas, but their dogs barked loudly. There were a great many dogs. Some were half in the water.

Others ran barking wildly among the Indians standing there.

David saw the fording place and urged his horse into the water.

"Jehosophat!" exclaimed Nate. "We ain't goin' right over there?"

"We sure are," answered David. "You watch out behind but don't get scared. Indians don't like to see anybody scared —especially a white man."

When they were in the middle of the river, hanging tight to their horses, Nate looked around and saw four Chippewas coming off the trail they had just left. David knew that some Indians would be following them. These Indians plunged into the river and followed them.

As they approached the opposite shore, the Chippewas ranged there parted and made way for them. The barking of the dogs increased in fury, but the Indians made no sign of greeting. Instead, they turned on the dogs and sent them howling away with kicks and blows.

David rode on to the land with his right hand upraised in the kind of greeting that the Indians always had used at the Claver home. Suydam and Nate raised their hands, too. The Indians had divided to make a path through the crowd. It led straight up into the open place among the lodges.

There, in front of his lodge, sat an old Indian who was the chieftain of the tribe. He wore more feathers on his head than the other braves did, and he was flanked by warriors. All stood except the old man, who, seeing the arms of the travelers aloft, slowly raised his own right hand.

Behind them now the other Indians came crowding into the open place. Some made so bold as to come close enough to touch the horses. All were curious, but none wished to risk the displeasure of the old chief by pressing too close to their visitors.

David slid off his horse. Suydam and Nate followed suit.

This was the most difficult part of their visit to the Chippewa village, for none of them could understand the Chippewa language. David knew a few words; Suydam knew a few others; Nate knew none at all. After the word of greeting, they would have to depend on sign language. And it was clear that Suydam would have to do the talking, because the old chief's eyes were fixed on him as the oldest of the three.

Suydam stepped forward and began to make signs to the chief.

One of the braves came forward, too. He stepped in front of Suydam and pointed to the old chief. "Black Rock," he said.

So the chief's name was Black Rock.

Suydam hoped that the brave could talk English, but he proved to know no more of that language than Suydam did of the Chippewa. He had learned the English name for his chief from a missionary. Nevertheless, among them, and with the aid of signs, they began to make talk.

Suydam explained that they were on the way to the "big water" in the north. The three of them were traveling on the order of "the white chief of the Michigan Territory."

As soon as this was made clear to Chief Black Rock, the old man broke into excited talk. When this had been translated into signs, it turned out to mean that the old man wished Suydam and his companions to tell the Governor they needed help. They were short of supplies. The winter had been bad.

Suydam turned to the pack-horse. He took from one of the packs a sack of tobacco and presented this to the chief.

Black Rock grinned with pleasure. He asked Suydam what he could do for them.

Suydam had two requests.

The first had to do with food. They had dipped deep into their store of provisions. They still had enough for three days travel, but if the Chippewas could spare some venison the travelers would be happy to have it.

The second had to do with another matter. David followed the signs with interest. Suydam asked whether any among these Indians knew the trails to the north water. He wanted a guide to the shore of the lake.

The problem of provisions was readily settled. In spite of the chief's lament for the Governor about needing help, the Chippewa village seemed to have plenty of food. Black Rock said they would exchange either fresh venison or dried meat for more tobacco, or perhaps some cloth, if the white travelers carried any.

But the matter of the guide was different. True, there was one among them who knew the trails into the north all the way to the great water, across from the Island of the Turtle. Did the white travelers mean to go to the Island of the Turtle?

Suydam said they meant to go in that direction.

Black Rock raised his voice in a shout. Then he settled back to wait. Everyone else waited, too, until a slender young brave came out of the crowd and stood before Black Rock.

The old chief waved toward their visitors and talked rapidly in the Chippewa language. The young brave answered. For some time they talked back and forth. Then the brave walked along the horses and put his hand on the pack-horse.

He felt the horses's legs. He looked at his teeth. After this, he returned and talked more with the chief.

Finally the chief turned again to Suydam. The sign language began once more.

Black Rock said that Flying Bird was willing to accompany the white men. He would lead them by the easiest trails to the edge of the great water in the north. But he would go no farther. In return, he would ask the white travelers to give him the horse they did not ride.

"The horse is too heavily laden to carry a man," answered Suydam.

"That is true now," agreed Black Rock. "But when you have finished your journey, you will have no more need of a horse to carry your packs. Then Flying Bird can ride him back to us."

Suydam did not know what to say. He tried to explain that they might need a pack-horse on the return journey just as well as on the trip north. But the chief did not seem to understand this. None of them seemed to understand, either because they did not wish to or because they did not believe him.

At last Suydam tried to say that they could go north without a guide. They had come this far without one. They could go the rest of the way by themselves.

Unhappily, the Chippewas did not seem to understand this, either. They muttered among themselves, and old Black Rock sat impassive not so much as a muscle of his face moving.

David began to chuckle.

Hearing him, Suydam, too, broke into a laugh. "I guess I let them trap me," he said.

"Yes, sir," agreed David.

Suydam turned to the old chief and gave in. He agreed that the guide should have the extra horse for his services.

Immediately the Indians' features thawed. Because they felt they had got the better of this white man in a bargain, they were as pleased with themselves as children. Black Rock clapped his hands and shouted orders for a feast to be laid for their visitors.

All Suydam's protests were in vain. The Indians had so much time they could not imagine anyone who had to hurry. They did not believe Suydam had to make haste.

"We'll have to stay, sir," said David. "Indians consider it bad manners—downright unfriendly—when white men don't accept anything they offer."

Suydam resigned himself to the delay. If only it had meant a meal and no more! But the Chippewas made a great ceremony out of everything, and the entertainment of visitors was no exception.

Flying Bird, after pausing once more to pat the horse which he would soon bring back to the village as his own, went to make ready for the journey.

XI.

THE ISLAND OF THE TURTLE

IT WAS LATE afternoon when they set out from the Chippewa village. Despite the approach of night, Suydam would not delay any longer. It made no difference to Flying Bird what time they started.

Flying Bird now led the way. Suydam followed, and the boys came after. The Indian went on foot. He traveled so fast that he was compelled to wait for the white men now and then.

When night came, Flying Bird simply curled up and slept on the ground, without covering of any kind.

Next morning, the Chippewa was up with the sun. When David woke, he found Flying Bird cleaning three squirrels he had shot.

"We have a hunter as well as a guide with us," said Suydam. "We'll have fresh meat every day."

When they started away after breakfast, Flying Bird promised to make good time before sundown. But he was baffled when Suydam ordered a halt scarcely an hour on the way, in order to survey and explore the land. He could not understand Suydam's instruments. He was consumed by curiosity about them. He wanted everything explained to him. Though he understood what Suydam said, he still did not grasp why it was necessary to do what Suydam was doing.

In his sign language, Flying Bird made his meaning clear. "Ground—good, grow corn," he said. "Many birds, many deer, many squirrels, many fish—plenty to eat. Plenty water. What more does the white man need?"

"The White Father in Detroit tells us to do this," explained Suydam. "He wishes to show it to the Great White Father in Washington."

Flying Bird left no one in any doubt that he thought white men were crazy.

They were now traveling through unbroken wilderness, moving steadily northward. Many times each day Suydam struck out away from the trail Flying Bird followed. Sometimes he was gone for as much as an hour at a time. Sometimes he insisted on following side trails which took them far out of the way.

David and Nate both learned how to use Suydam's instruments. The surveyor taught them how to judge the nature of the soil, as well.

Not to be outdone, Flying Bird taught the boys how to study trails and how to follow the tracks of men or animals in the wilderness. He taught them how to recognize animal and bird signs, as well as approaching changes in the weather.

They traveled through all kinds of weather. They did not stop for rain or storm. As they went along, they continued to look for more Indian villages, but they saw none.

"I thought there'd be more Indian towns," said Nate one day when they paused to eat.

"I understood from Governor Mason that most of the Indians live near the lake shore or up a river not far from the lake," answered Suydam. "Besides, many of them have moved west. As white men come into the country, the Indians move farther west still—as soon as they sell their land."

"I thought they took it away from the Indians," said Nate.

"Sometimes that happens, too. But mostly the government buys it. Then the surveyors go to work, and as the settlers come, the land offices open."

As they moved into the north, they found more and more lakes. At the same time, the country grew more rolling, and occasional high hills began to make their appearance.

On the morning of their twentieth day from the Chippewa village, they woke to a light west wind blowing. Flying Bird appeared to be very joyful. He pointed to his nose and pretended to take a deep breath.

"What's he trying to tell us now?" asked Nate.

"He wants us to smell the air," answered David. "Don't you smell it?"

"It's fresh."

"It's the lake smell. He's telling us we're close to where he agreed to guide us."

They no longer had to depend on Flying Bird's signs. In the days they had spent with him, they had learned many

Chippewa words. They could now talk with Flying Bird about most simple events of each day.

So when David asked whether they were not soon coming to the "big water", Flying Bird said that they were. He explained that, if "the man with the measuring sticks"—which was his name for Suydam—did not stop too often, they would reach the lake by mid-day.

By early afternoon, they could see the lake. As soon as they came within sight of the shore, Flying Bird stopped. He would go no farther.

"Big water," he said, pointing.

Then he went around to the pack horse and stood with the palm of his hand laid against the horse's flank. "I go," he said.

Suydam did not argue with Flying Bird, even though they were not yet at Lake Huron. He dismounted at once. The boys followed suit. They began the task of distributing the burden carried by the pack-horse among the other horses.

As soon as this was finished, Flying Bird mounted the pack-horse. He sat there awkwardly with an expession of pleasure on his usually stolid face. Then he made a farewell sign and turned back along the trail. He fell off almost as soon as the horse moved.

Suydam quieted Nate's laughter sharply. "Don't offend him, Nate. He's not used to riding. Very probably he never rode a horse before. They say only the western Indians—the Sioux beyond the Mississippi—have horses."

"And all the rest want them," added David.

Flying Bird remounted, sitting as awkwardly as before. Then he was on his way again. He fell off a second time before he found a way to keep his seat on the horse's broad back.

Soon he was out of sight.

"Which way now?" asked Nate.

Suydam pointed north. A large island lay along the horizon in the blue waters of Lake Huron. "That will be part of the Territory," he said. "We have no orders to stop at the lake's edge."

"I don't think the horses could swim that far," said Nate seriously.

Suydam laughed. "Can you handle a canoe, Nate?"

"Yes, sir. Not too well—but I've used a paddle."

"I can learn," said David.

"The only thing is," Nate went on, "where's the canoe?"

David grinned. "Smell that smoke, Nate? Sure as shooting, there's an Indian camp around."

"Let's find it," said Suydam.

It was more than a camp. It was a village of Ottawa Indians on the lake shore.

This time their approach was unobserved. The Ottawas had lived for so long knowing visitors only from the lake, that they had no longer watched so carefully by land. The travelers were not seen until they were almost upon the village. Then a group of Indian boys, playing at the edge of the town, saw them and ran back into the settlement, shouting warnings.

Ottawas appeared at once from all directions. They came out of their lodges and sprang up from the lake shore. There they all stood, surrounded by barking dogs. They were astonished at the sight of white men coming on horses. They stared as if at a sight they had never seen before.

Suydam's horse was almost upon them before they parted to let them through.

The Ottawa chieftain was not in the village. He was on a visit to the Island of the Turtle, which was Mackinac. They were received instead by some of the lesser chiefs.

Once more Suydam had to resort to sign language.

He explained patiently that he wanted to go to the Island of the Turtle. But whenever he pointed out toward the land in the waters of Lake Huron, there was a vigorous head-shaking among the chiefs. All wanted to talk at once. Since none had any more authority than the other, there was no one to lead in the talk.

But at last they made it clear to Suydam that the island to which he pointed was the Island of the White Wood. Mackinac was beyond it, farther toward the north, in the straits between Lake Huron and Lake Michigan.

This understood, they went on to barter for a canoe which would take the three travelers and their belongings not only to Mackinac but perhaps beyond it. It must be a strong, seasoned canoe, one which would stand up against the "white water" of rapids as well as the lake.

Suydam began by offering one horse in exchange for a canoe. But both he and the Indians knew that he could not take the remaining two horses by canoe to Mackinac. He would have to leave them here. From one horse, Suydam went to two. He had every intention of offering the three horses to the Ottawas in exchange for a canoe, but he wanted the Indians to feel that they had got the best of a bargain.

After much talk back and forth, the Ottawas agreed to permit Suydam to select his own canoe from among those along the lake shore. The chiefs led the three travelers and their horses to the canoes.

As soon as Suydam had made his choice, all the Ottawas helped enthusiastically to load the canoe.

This done, Suydam turned again to the chiefs. "Now I must have materials to repair the canoe if we need to repair it," he told them by signs, "I want many things."

This request seemed to the Ottawas only reasonable. They brought all the things Suydam asked for—fine roots of young spruce trees, called *wattap* by the Indians, with which to sew the birch bark on to the gunwales of the canoe—pitch pine— extra paddles—bundles of bark. To the Indians, any request now would be filled, for the three horses were of far more value to them than one canoe.

The baggage was packed at both ends of the canoe and covered with the same oil-cloth that had covered it on the horse, in case of rain or waves washing up. Suydam sat near the baggage at one end, and Nate at the other. David sat in the middle, but not before Suydam had warned him about the delicate balance of a canoe, and how easily it could be upset.

With the Indians crowded down to see them off, they pushed out into the lake. The Ottawas shouted their farewells. Some of them capered about. Still others began to move toward the horses.

As the land receded behind them, and water loomed on all sides, David thought of the farm he had left, of his brothers and sisters and his parents. How far away they seemed now! Even Toledo had been almost in the neighborhood compared to where they were now. How different it was to be out on so vast an expanse of water, after the weeks of travel in the wilderness!

For the first time, David wondered whether he would ever see home again.

But he had little time to look backward. The canoe sped through the water. Yet, while the mainland receded behind them, the island ahead did not seem to grow nearer. They were heading toward the Island of the White Wood. From the western end of this island, the Ottawas had told them, they could see the Island of the Turtle.

David marvelled at Nate's ability to handle the paddle. He had not known that Nate was accomplished in this way. He resolved to learn just as soon as he could. Perhaps, once they were at Mackinac, Suydam would let Nate teach him how to paddle.

As each hour passed, Mackinac seemed farther away. Though the Island of the White Wood began to loom closer, the day was also rapidly drawing to an end. The sun was a great flaming ball low over the water to the west. David knew, because of his hunger, that it was already past the supper hour. He reckoned that it must be close to eight o'clock, for the month was June, and the days were long.

At last they rounded the western tip of the Island of the White Wood. Mackinac lay just ahead. In the sunset glow they could see the white cliffs and the stone fortress that crowned them showing just above the surface of the water.

They rode into the crescent-shaped harbor of Mackinac in the soft twilight. The afterglow was still bright. It fanned up into the western sky, and a cusp of new moon lay pale there.

Before them rose a village of log houses and some buildings which belonged to the American Fur Company. At the fort, above the village, light twinkled like stars against the darkening heavens. Above the roofs of the houses a spire of a church rose up, and, near at hand, the masts of ships drawn up in the harbor.

The sight of the quiet village, with so many windows yellow with lights, filled David with a longing for home. It was almost a month since they had been in a settlement of white men. That had been Saginaw—and how far away that city seemed! David could tell, by Nate's silence, that Nate felt much the same way he did. Perhaps even more so—for Nate was used to living in Detroit.

Suydam, however, was all excitement. "We'll draw the canoe up on the beach," he said. "I have a number of things to do here. I want to talk with the *voyageurs* who travel north. I want to see a map of their trails, if they have such a thing. What do you say to my finding you a bed for the night?"

"No, sir," both boys answered at once. "We're used to sleeping outside, and somebody'll have to stay at the canoe," added David.

"It would probably be safe, unless the Indians found it. But, look, as soon as we land, why don't you stretch your legs in Mackinac town, and I'll wait here until you come back."

To this the boys agreed.

They beached the canoe away from the harbor and drew it out of the water. Then the boys walked into the village.

Mackinac town was built below the fort, along the shore of the island, which rose up behind it and shone out across the water very much like the Turtle to which Indians and *voyageurs* compared it. The town was neat and orderly, unlike most settlements in Michigan. This was because it was much older than other towns in the Territory.

As they walked up and down, the boys said little. Each was

lost in his own thoughts. David was filled with wonder at how large the Michigan Territory was. So far away from home, and, according to Suydam, they were not yet half way to the western edge of the Territory! He thought, too, of the little farm west of Detroit, and from what Nate did say from time to time, it was plain that he was comparing Detroit to Mackinac. Neither of them had ever been so far away from home alone before.

Darkness had fallen when they returned to where Suydam waited. Suydam was anxious to be off. He waited only to make sure that David and Nate would not take a bed somewhere in the village, if he could find one. Then, on their repeated refusal, he left, promising to be back as soon as he could. He promised to bring food from the shops for them if they wanted a change from the supplies.

But long before Suydam returned, David and Nate had eaten and gone to sleep, one on each side of the canoe, like guardians.

XII.

NORTH TO LAKE SUPERIOR

B<small>Y MORNING</small>, all was in readiness for their journey north of the Island of the Turtle.

In the night, Suydam had gathered supplies. He had carried them from Mackinac town down to the canoe and packed them. He had brought dried beef, corn meal, bacon, sugar, and other food. He had bought gum to patch the canoe, and other things they might need. The canoe was now somewhat crowded.

In addition, Suydam had acquired a rough map of their route.

"I called in at the American Fur Company office," he explained. "The *voyageurs* would know the routes better than anyone else. Come and see how far the Territory extends."

David and Nate bent over the map he unfolded.

"Here's Mackinac—and this is the way we'll go," said Suydam, tracing with his finger. "We must follow the shore and stay close enough so we can go ashore at once if we get heavy weather. We leave Lake Huron east of where we are now, go into the straits of St. Mary. Then up the St. Mary River. There's the Sault. That's the most northern settlement in the Michigan Territory. Across the river from it lies Canada. And up the river is Lake Superior. That's where we're going."

"And then?" asked David.

"Then we follow the south shore of Lake Superior almost to the end of the lake—if we have time. All this land south of the lake down to the border of Illinois is Michigan Territory."

"Do you mean we're aimin' to cover it all?" put in Nate.

Suydam's eyes danced with merriment at Nate's alarm. "We couldn't," he answered. "Not any more this year. We'd end up frozen in somewhere. And the Governor's too anxious for a report to wait that long. We'll just go as far west as we can—up a few rivers and back to the lake. We'll explore and survey where it suits us. Then we'll come back."

"Whew!" exclaimed Nate with relief. "For a minute you had me scared."

David tried to imagine how long it would take them. Three days to the Sault, at the least. Another day for Lake Superior. Beyond that he did not try to guess. It would be many weeks—perhaps months—before they would be home again.

"What do you say, Nate?" asked Suydam. "Do you think

David's ready for a turn at the paddle today? The water's quiet and the air calm."

"I reckon so," answered Nate. "I can sit in the middle and watch him—unless you want to rest, Mr. Suydam."

"I'd like to try, sir," said David.

"Then it's settled."

They carried the canoe back to the water.

Now that morning was well advanced, they could see how busy the harbor of Mackinac was. Ships, large and small, were in the harbor. There were also many canoes. Some of these were decorated with the gay colors of the *voyageurs*— the daring employees of the fur companies who went far and wide to trade for furs and bring them to Mackinac. But most of the canoes belonged to Indian travelers.

In addition to those in the harbor, there were many other canoes on the water, out in the lake. Some were moving out from Mackinac; they went north and east. They went southeast and southwest. They went directly across to the mainland on both sides of the Island of the Turtle. Some were moving in toward the harbor. All traveled very swiftly.

At first the paddle in his hands made David feel awkward. What had seemed to him so smooth and easy a motion, when he had watched Nate handling the paddle, now seemed clumsy. He felt stiff and he was convinced that he was only holding Suydam back.

Once or twice Suydam looked back to smile encouragement.

"That's it, Dave," Nate kept saying. "That's the way. Just get the feel of it—that's all."

At first David believed that Nate was only trying to give him courage, because he did not belive he would ever feel at ease with the paddle in his hands and the responsibility that went with it. But then, gradually, surprisingly, a feeling of confidence crept into him, and slowly he grew more sure of himself. The canoe sped forward despite the clumsiness he felt. David could see that, novice or not, his paddling was not holding them back. The paddle seemed lighter, and his movements more smooth.

After the first two hours, David hardly thought about paddling at all. It now seemed easy and natural for him, as if he had been doing it a long time. He settled himself for the long pull ahead.

On the fourth day from Mackinac, they reached the Sault. They had lost a day when a storm drove them to shore for five hours, and when Suydam decided they should not risk more of the rapids of the St. Mary River than necessary. Their small craft in any but experienced hands could easily be so badly damaged as to be beyond repair. For that reason, they portaged some lengths which other travelers took by water. They carried the canoe along the shore of the St. Mary for a greater distance than most other travelers, who carried for only the last half mile, where the river foamed over treacherous rocks.

The Sault de Sainte Marie seemed to David a very large settlement. It rose on a plateau on the American side of the river. There was a garrison of soldiers there at the fort. There were also bark cabins, log houses, some frame houses, some stone buildings, and many lodges. Then David saw that what he had thought part of the village was actually a large settlement of Chippewa Indians, whose lodges reached almost back to the woods. They were separated from the village by Fort Brady, which stood out bright in its white among the dun-

colored buildings all around. Beyond the green grass around
the fort were extensive gardens.

Leaving Nate with the canoe, Suydam and David went into
the village. Suydam made directly for the distinctive buildings which bore the sign of the American Fur Company.

An aging man, rough in appearance, greeted them in the
office. He was grizzled and wore the look of a man who had
spent much of his life under the sun in the open. But his eyes
were clear and youthful, and the long hair he wore showed
only a little grey.

Suydam introduced himself and David.

"Gabriel Franchere, at your service," said the old man.
"What can I do for you?"

Suydam explained that they were three amateur travelers.
"You might call us greenhorns," he said. He outlined the
course he hoped to take into the west.

To all this Franchere listened gravely. When Suydam
finished, he said only that there was little he could tell
him. "The Indians you'll meet there are friendly—there are
still quite a few of them. Some have gone west into Sioux
country. They'll expect something in the way of gifts—at
least, the chiefs will. But a little tobacco or a knife will do."

"We're carrying both."

Franchere cautioned them about the route along the south
shore of Lake Superior. "There are dangerous cliffs and rocks
—steer clear of them. Then there's the weather, too—it's
always changeable and stormy about the time of the solstice."

Suydam thanked him.

"A surveyor, eh?" continued Franchere. "You may find
some interesting things in that country, Mr. Suydam. We

hear many reports—but we never know how much belief to put into them."

Suydam's interest was immediately excited. "What kind of reports?" he asked.

"They don't bear repeating unless we can be sure," said Franchere.

Suydam tried another tack. "Do the Indians ever bring in any metal, sir?"

The agent grinned. "The Indians have metal, Mr. Suydam."

This was apparently what Suydam wanted to know. He exchanged a little more small talk with Franchere, then bade him farewell.

David waited in vain for Suydam to explain his interest in the metal the Indians might have. But Suydam said nothing. He walked along without saying a word. David concluded finally that this was perhaps another line of inquiry the Governor had suggested.

Now they were ready to go on from the Sault to the vastness of that wilderness which lay to the west.

On the day after they left the Sault, the river led them into a deep bay which connected to Lake Superior. On both sides of the water here were towering peaks. Ahead stretched a limitless expanse of deep blue water. At the horizon, the water vanished into a kind of haze and became sky.

They followed along the south shore of the bay, making a great arc until they came to a point of land pushing out into the water. There they turned into the southwest.

Now they were on the greatest of the lakes. They were passing by high ridges, covered with dense forests. The shore seemed to be rocky, and sometimes a pebbled beach could be seen. Suydam kept watch for the mouth of any stream, but he saw none.

David was awed by the wildness and vastness of lake and land in this place. How completely it differed from the little homestead west of Detroit! Despite the washing sounds of the water, there was a great stillness which brooded over everything. Birds flew along the shore, but made no cry. No wind stirred. Only the silent birds and the great rolling water seemed alive.

They traveled as close to shore as Suydam thought safe. Once they pushed to land, so that Suydam could surrender his paddle to Nate. After that, Suydam sat in the middle of the canoe, watching the shore. The hills slowly grew lower, and the forests grew more dense.

Though paddling in the lake was much easier than paddling against the St. Mary's current, David and Nate were both tired of the kneeling position in which they paddled by the time Suydam called a halt. He had at last seen the mouth of a river emptying into the lake.

"In we go, boys, and up stream," he ordered.

The river was but a small one. Nevertheless, its current was swift and its water deep. They moved up river until Suydam gave the signal to land. Then they drove in to shore, to spend their first night under the old trees which crowded down to the water's edge on both sides of the stream and on much of the shore of the lake. The sun was already going down, and all were tired and hungry.

"You can sleep as long as you like in the morning, boys," promised Suydam, as they sat about their evening meal.

"We'll want to take time to look around whenever we come in off the lake."

"You won't find much here," said Nate, looking around. "Just woods as far's a man can see."

"The woods might hide a lot of things, Nate," answered Suydam.

"How far do you figure we are from home?" asked Nate then.

"I wish I could tell you. Over three hundred miles as the crow flies, I'd guess. Probably closer to four hundred. Of course, we've traveled more than that."

"And we're not done traveling, either," added David.

Suydam smiled. "Anybody for home? We could always stop somebody going toward the Sault."

Neither David nor Nate spoke up. Tired as they were, each was happy to be here in the heart of this great wilderness. And, though each thought of home with longing, neither was yet ready to turn his back upon such adventures as might lie ahead.

When David woke next morning, he was astonished to find that Suydam was gone. He leaned over and poked Nate.

"Nate! Wake up! Mr. Suydam's gone," he cried.

Nate rolled over. He stretched and sat up, blinking. He looked at Suydam's empty place, then at David, puzzled. Then he glanced toward the river.

"The canoe!" he cried.

The canoe was gone, too.

For a few moments the boys were filled with alarm. Then the peacefulness of the summer morning affected them. The songs of the birds, the quiet voice of the water, the light wind rustling the leaves overhead combined to soothe them.

"He's probably just gone up the river," said David. "He said we'd look around some. He said we could sleep longer today." He looked toward the sun and added, "It must be all of nine o'clock."

"We sure slept," said Nate. "And I'm hungry as a bear, too."

Nevertheless, despite their reassurance, the boys spent an uneasy hour. They gathered up their utensils. They packed their robes and blankets. Then they gathered ripe berries which grew along the river bank and ate them.

"What kind of berries are these?" asked Nate.

"Raspberries," answered David.

"I never paid much mind to such stuff," said Nate. "I guess it's different living in a city. If I ever take to farming, like I kind of figure on doin', I'd better find out a lot."

"You've found out a lot already, Nate. All about the different kinds of soil and stone, the trees and the grasses. You've got a good start."

An hour later, Suydam came downstream in the canoe and edged gently in to land. He stepped lightly out of the canoe.

"I hope you boys weren't scared," he said. "I went up river a way."

"No, sir," said David. "We didn't think you got lost."

"Or ran out on us," added Nate, grinning.

"I should have told you. But you were sleeping so soundly I thought it would be a shame to wake you. Besides, I planned to make it back before you woke. Are you rested?"

"Yes, sir. Had breakfast, too. Ready to go on."

"Then let's be on our way."

They had not been on the lake more than three hours when

Suydam once again sent them landward. A broader river mouth than any yet seen along Lake Superior opened up invitingly at that place.

Once more they entered into a world of green. In some places along the river the trees almost arched together, so that they moved along under a canopy of leaves. They went with care. Many trees had fallen into the water, and these had to be avoided lest the bark of the canoe be torn.

Every little while, Suydam motioned them to bear shoreward. Sometimes he got out to examine the stones in the shallow water along the water's edge. Sometimes he walked into the woods and was gone for half an hour or more. Most of the time he returned to the canoe disappointed, but once, after he had examined stones along the water line, he brought some back to the canoe with him.

He held them in his palms for the boys to see. They were discolored. A reddish-brown color seemed to have been painted on them.

"Looks like iron deposits," said Suydam.

He kept the stones.

As they turned back toward the lake again, Suydam said, "This is what we'll be doing for days and weeks ahead. Until we get tired of hunting food or fishing for it. Tired of looking at ground and hills, at woods and stones, sky and water. We'll be a long way from home then—and we'll be a lot more tired of sky and water before we get back. We'll be on water from now until Detroit once more."

David whistled. "That's easy a thousand miles," he guessed.

"Easy," agreed the surveyor.

XIII.

RENEGADES

As the days turned into weeks, David lost track of them. They moved steadily westward. But no day was ever exactly like another. While it was true that the surveyor followed the same pattern, each day was different. Sometimes storms drove them in off the lake. Once they were slow to move and were almost dashed to pieces on the rocks. After that, the slightest rise in the force of the wind sent them hurrying to land and safe cover.

Sometimes they took half a day off their quest to hunt. Deer abounded here, and they never had any trouble keeping their supplies of meat to eat. Berries could be found everywhere, and Suydam knew succulent leaves they could add to their diet. Now and then they fished, but this was hardly sport, for the fish were so plentiful that they leaped at whatever bait was offered them.

Hardly a day went by on the lake that they did not pass travelers heading for the Sault. Once they were overtaken by couriers on their way to the Grand Portage at the western end of Lake Superior. From them they learned that the people of Detroit were stirring things up in their eagerness to join the Union as a new State, and that the militias of Michigan Territory and Ohio were still drawn up along the disputed area of land. Not a shot had been fired since David and Nate had left.

Lake travelers included *voyageurs, coureurs de bois*—travelers of the woods—Indians, fur-traders, *engagés*—hired men who paddled and guided travelers—officers of the fur companies, soldiers, and now and then a daring traveler looking for new country in which to settle. Most of the travelers stopped to talk; only now and then an official hastened past with only a wave of the hand and the raised paddles which were the greetings of the *voyageurs*.

They traveled past scenery of great beauty. There were high walls of sandstone, showing many colors. There were rocky shores that stretched for miles. Sometime falls of water fell into the lake from off cliffs and out of clefts in the rocks. They paddled past high bluffs which were orange and claret, brown, yellow and green. The bluffs had caves in them, and were broken by small bays. They went under rocky arches which filled David and Nate with awe. Often they went for miles along the shore only to find that they had followed an isthmus, and must now return down its far side.

Often when they went inland along the rivers, as well as

when they camped for the night along the lake shore, they met Indians. They were always Chippewas. There were many more of them here along Lake Superior than there had been in the Territory between Saginaw City and Mackinac. The Chippewas were all friendly. They always tried to make some kind of trade, and they were usually satisfied with any trinket or gift Suydam offered them, as if it were the spirit of trading which was important to them, and not the objects of the trade. Sometimes the Indians provided guides for Suydam when he struck out away from the river, but, since most of them lived close to the lake shore, this did not often happen.

Though the lure of adventure did not lessen for the boys, both were beginning to look forward to their return journey. David was sure that the Governor could ask no more than that which Suydam could now tell him—that the Michigan Territory was far richer than anyone had supposed, least of all the government surveyor who had made so unfavorable a report about it to Washington. Yet Suydam drove relentlessly on.

One day they entered a broad river of a strange rust color. The sight of it excited Suydam.

"We'll go up here as far as we can," he said. "This looks like iron country. We've already found traces of it. There's no telling what we may discover in the interior."

At the moment, it was David's turn to ride the middle of the canoe. It was he who saw what looked at first like an obstruction across the river. Even as he pointed at it, he saw what it was.

"Why, it's a dam!" he cried.

As they drew near, Suydam identified it. "It's all that's

left of an old fishing weir. The Indians built them and fished from them. They always left a passage on one side. This one has broken out on both."

They made their way past the remains of the weir. Rounding a bend just above it, they came upon a Chippewa encampment. There were only a dozen Chippewas, and no buildings were to be seen.

"A hunting party," said David at once.

The Indians had seen them. They came crowding down to the shore.

"We'll land," said Suydam.

The Chippewas laid hands on the canoe as soon as it touched shore and helped to pull it well up on land. All made the traditional signs of friendship. Then the young chief who led the party stepped forward.

Suydam greeted them in the Chippewa language. Then, by a mixture of signs and words he had learned from other Chippewas, he and the young chief talked.

The chief, whose name was Night Cloud, told him they were in the country of the Ontonagon. He seemed anxious to knew how far the white travelers intended to go.

"As far as we can up river," answered Suydam.

Night Cloud shook his head. "Do not go," he said. "There are renegade Indians. Bad Indians. Do not go. Besides, you cannot go all the way up the river. It grows too narrow for the canoe. There are many rocks and trees in the water."

"How far are we from the Great Father of Waters?" asked Suydam.

Night Cloud motioned to the west. "Far, far. Many days. One moon—perhaps two."

Suydam presented Night Cloud with the last of the tobacco he carried. Night Cloud thanked him, and in turn gave Suydam a hunting knife. Then Suydam stepped back to the canoe and pushed it back out toward the river. Before he stepped into it, he stooped to pick up some of the rust-colored pebbles along the river's edge. Then he got into the canoe.

The Chippewas ran forward to push the canoe out into the river.

As they moved south, Suydam told them what the Chippewas had said. "I don't put much faith in their talk about renegade Indians," he added. "It's possible, but I doubt that we'll get up that far. The question now is what to do. We can't make it to the Mississippi. It's the middle of July now. It would be late August by the best time we could make. By September there'll be sharp weather changes to face in this north country."

"We'll do whatever you think best, sir," said David.

"But what do you think, boys?"

"I think we can't find out much more for Governor Mason," said David promptly. "He wouldn't ask for more. We know how much timber is here, and how rich the land is all over the Territory."

"There's iron, too," put in Nate.

"And something more he'll be glad to have brought to his attention," said Suydam, throwing some of the pebbles he had picked up so that they fell on the oilcloth between the boys. "I'm sure that's copper. It's copper that colors this river, not iron!" He grinned with pleasure at the discovery. "And as soon as I've made sure of it, we start back."

They went steadily up the river until the channel narrowed. Then they camped for the night.

They had now reached more open country. It was not prairie, nor yet an area of oak openings, but one less densely forested. It was a country broken by ravines and rocky ridges among occasional deep woods extending from the forests which made an unbroken line to the lake's edge now miles away.

Suydam guessed they could not be far from the source of the mineral deposit which colored the water of the river. Perhaps next day they would find it. His talk pleased the boys, since they knew that they would soon begin the journey homeward.

They turned in early, filled with hope for the morrow.

In the morning, Suydam was gone again. David and Nate were not alarmed, since Suydam was often awake long before them, and out on his own, exploring the country. Sometimes he came back and took both of them with him for a deeper penetration of the wilderness. Most of the time, though, he was tired when he got back, and content to get into the canoe and go on.

After breakfast, the boys swam for a while in the rust-colored water. The water was cool, even for July. Then they found a place in the sun and lay there, tanning themselves.

Mid-morning came and went. There was no sign of Suydam.

In another hour, David began to grow uneasy. "He's never been gone this long before, Nate. What did he take with him?"

"His instruments and his gun," said Nate, after he had looked among Suydam's things. "Can't see that any food's gone."

"Then he ought to be back by this time," said David.

"S'pose something's happened to him, Dave?"

"I hope not," answered David fervently.

"I reckon we better go see. But which way did he go?"

"That won't be had to find out," said David confidently.

He began to walk in widening arcs from the shore of the river on one side of their camp to the shore on the other side. Now all he had learned from Flying Bird on their journey up from Saginaw served him well. In a little while he came to the plain marks of Suydam's walking from camp.

"He went south," he said. "Up the river."

"Well, let's go after him," proposed Nate.

"Just a minute, Nate. If something's happened to Mr. Suydam, we'll have to be ready for it. We'll need knives and guns. If he fell and broke a leg, we'll have to make a litter."

"Maybe an animal's got him treed. Remember—we saw bears on the way up this river."

"But we can hardly take more than guns and knives, or we won't be able to make any time," continued David.

"Let's go, Dave. He can't be far away."

They started away from camp fully armed. But they did not go until they had pulled the canoe back into the woods and hidden it under branches. The trail, once David pointed it out to Nate, was not hard to follow. A footstep here—a broken twig there—turned leaves and blades in another place —a trampled flower—all these indications could not be mistaken. The trail led up along the river. It was plain to see that every little while Suydam had gone to the river to pick up a stone or look at a rock. But always he had come back to resume the trail.

Now and then their way led through tall grass. Here Suydam's trail was very easy to follow. Sometimes the two boys could fairly race along. Then again, there were times when they had to study the ground closely, or circle until they came upon traces again.

It was past noon before they stopped to rest.

"How far are we from camp, do you reckon, Dave?" asked Nate.

"Between three and four miles, I'd say."

"He wouldn't go much farther than this."

"I don't think he would."

"Maybe he cut in from the river and got back to camp. Maybe he's there now, wondering what happened to us?"

David smiled ruefully. "I guess he'd say it would serve us right—not to trust him. We'll go on though, just the same—as long as we can see a trail."

Half an hour after they had set out once more, the trail ended abruptly in a place where there was evidence to show that more than one man had been there. There were broken branches all around. There were pieces of sod kicked loose. What was most telling of all was the sight of a little measuring stick which was Suydam's. There it lay, mutely, on the grass.

"Something happened here," said Nate gravely. "Looks like a fight."

David was already on his knees, carefully examining the ground. He began to circle the area, Nate on his heels. Almost at once they came upon a trail leading west. It was a broad trail, made by more than one traveler. It led straight through a band of trees toward an open place. There the grass was all trampled down. When the trail took up again, its nature had changed—there were hoofprints to be seen.

"Three men, three horses," said David, after studying the ground and the new trail. "Another man walking."

"That'd be Mr. Suydam," ventured Nate. "They're going west—away from the river. Why didn't he warn us?"

David looked at him soberly. "I'm afraid it's pretty serious, Nate. It looks like Indians."

"But Indians hereabouts don't use horses. They don't own any," protested Nate. "Leastways, we never saw any horses near the villages."

"That's the worst of it, Nate," answered David. "We're getting into the West. That's Sioux country. And the Sioux do have horses. Remember what Night Cloud said to Mr. Suydam? About renegades? Renegades are Indians who have either left their tribe or been thrown out. They're no good."

"What would they want with Mr. Suydam?" asked Nate.

David shrugged. "I don't know. Maybe they figure on taking him back to the tribe and using him like a peace offering to get in again. Indians do queer things. They're not like us."

"Well," said Nate stoutly, "we're two, and they're only three. We'll have to go after them."

David nodded. "We'll have to be careful. They've got a head start on us. I don't know how much. The ground they kicked up isn't dry yet. It didn't take us as long to get here as it did Mr. Suydam. Maybe they're three hours ahead. And they can't go any faster than we can as long as Mr. Suydam has to walk. They'll go fast at first. Then they'll slow down— maybe hunt—maybe make camp."

"Come on," said Nate.

They set out in a loping run along the trail left by the horsemen.

Just before sundown, David stopped suddenly, holding up a hand to stop Nate, who was behind him.

"I smell smoke," said David.

Nate smelled the wind, which came from the west. "So do I."

"That means they've stopped for the night. From here on, we'll have to watch every step."

They pressed forward, taking advantage of every shelter, so that no sentinel could see them. They had been afraid for a while that they would not overtake Suydam and his captors, but, after finding a place on the trail where the Indians had stopped to hunt, the boys had regained confidence. Now they were sure their quarry was within reach.

The trail of the smoke was easy to follow. It was not even necessary for them to stay on the trail made by the horses. They deserted it and made their way by creeping and crawling through a belt of woods north of the trail. The smell of the smoke grew steadily stronger.

Finally David stopped and motioned to Nate to come up.

"I'm going on alone, Nate. If I don't come back, you're on your own. We've got to get Suydam back; so he can reach the Governor."

"How long shall I wait?" asked Nate anxiously.

"Give me an hour and a half. They can't be very far ahead."

"Dave—take care of yourself."

They spoke in whispers. Each was aware that danger

loomed just ahead of them. David smiled. He held out his
hand and Nate clasped it, hard. Then he slipped away and
vanished into the woods ahead. Not a leaf whispered, not a
twig snapped to show where he had gone. He had learned
well what Flying Bird had taught him so casually.

XIV.

RESCUE

Davⁱⁿ CAME WITHIN sight of the Sioux camp in fifteen minutes. The sounds of the horses reached him first. Then he heard the voices of the Indians, talking gutturally. He did not know their language. The smoke at this place swept low through the woods. Several times David had to choke back a cough. He crept resolutely ahead, maneuvering for a position from which he could see without being seen.

He found it at last, behind a growth of low scrub. He could look among the slender boles of the shrubs and see past the tree-trunks to where the fire burned. The Sioux were gathered around the fire. One was busy roasting some of the game they had taken. All three were talking excitedly.

But where was Suydam?

David peered from one side to the other. Then he saw Suydam's hands. No wonder he could not see him! Suydam was tied to a tree with leather thongs, and the tree was between David and the Indians. All he could see was Suydam's hands. Now and then he caught a glimpse of his feet. But Suydam could not move either hands or feet very much, for both were tied stoutly.

What could he do? David wondered, as he lay in his leafy shelter.

He tried to guess what the Sioux might do next. He gazed at them with interest, even though he was fully aware of his danger. They were fierce-looking Indians. They were not as well dressed as most of the Chippewas. They looked as if they had been wandering in the woods for many weeks. Perhaps that was just what they had been doing. They wore no paint, and they were almost without ornaments, not even feathers on the bands two of them had on. They were stocky and bronze, not lean and hard, but in the wan light of the setting sun, they looked menacing.

The fire—the roasting meat, which was surely venison, for the hunting place the boys had come upon had shown signs of a deer killed—the tethered horses—even Suydam tied to a tree—all these seemed to say to David that the Sioux were planning to stay here for the night.

Satisfied of this, David backed away from his post and made his way in the gathering dusk back to where Nate waited.

Nate was glad to see him.

David told him what he had seen, keeping his voice very low.

"What do we do, Dave?" asked Nate.

"We'll go back and wait. Two of them will go to sleep, sure. The other one might stand watch. Maybe all three will sleep. We can sneak up and cut Mr. Suydam loose, all right. We may have to wait half the night, though. But remember —not a sound. Indians can hear things you and I would miss by a mile."

"We'd better figure it out now, Dave. If we talked—they might hear us back there."

"I guess that's right. Tell you what we'll do. You plan on staying there with the gun all ready—just in case—and I'll cut him loose when the right time comes . . ."

Nate immediately objected. "What if you're in the way when I might have to fire?" He shook his head. "That's not the way. If there's a guard, I'll creep up on him and bash his head in with a rock . . ."

But this, too, did not seem the best plan. All kinds of problems seemed to go with any attempt to make a plan. They would have to depend on circumstances they might not be able to foresee.

"We'll just wait," said David. "We'll see what it looks like. We don't have to talk except by signs. Once we get Mr. Suydam cut lose, we can figure out something."

David led the way back to the Sioux camp.

Soon the two of them lay behind the scrub growth, watching the Indians. The Sioux were eating now. They tore at the roasted venison with strong teeth. They paid little attention to their captive. All three sat or crouched around the fire. Now that the sun had gone down, and darkness was beginning to cover the earth, the glow of the fire danced on the Sioux's bronze faces.

The boys lay in perfect quiet. But their very stillness was a test of their endurance, for mosquitoes they could not brush away found and stung them. There were constant rustlings in the woods. David could not tell what made all of them, though he knew the movements of rabbits and shrews and mice. Owls and whippoorwills began to call. Crickets started to churr, and the sawing of katydids rose with the constant humming of the mosquitoes.

Soon the darkness was complete, except for the light of an almost full moon riding high in the east. The fire died down, and the coals glowed for a little while in the moonlit darkness. Still the Sioux paid little attention to Suydam. One of them took a chunk of meat and held it in front of Suydam, with a guttural grunt.

David could not see clearly what was taking place. He guessed that Suydam was being offered food.

But Suydam apparently refused it.

The Sioux stood before him briefly. Then he grunted again and withdrew the meat.

Now the Indians began to make ready to sleep.

Two of them stretched out with their feet toward the coals, but far enough away so as to feel no heat, for the summer night was warm. The third sat cross-legged near Suydam.

Now and then this Sioux spoke to Suydam.

Suydam made no answer, at least none that David or Nate could hear. Perhaps he nodded or shook his head; this they could not see.

Once, the Indian got to his feet, walked over, and slapped Suydam. Evidently he was irritated at Suydam's silence. Then he went back to the fire, stirred and scattered the coals, and returned to be near Suydam.

Presently he, too, stretched out. Soon, like the others, he was asleep.

Each of the Sioux, David noticed, slept with his gun beside him. But only one of the guns seemed new. David concluded that this must be Suydam's gun. Since it lay beside the last of the Sioux to go to sleep, it must mean that this Sioux was Suydam's personal captor. Perhaps the others had no share in him.

David wondered whether Suydam was asleep. He could not see, but Suydam could hardly sleep in his position. The surveyor must be tired and acutely uncomfortable, since he had walked all day. What would he do if and when he was freed? This began to worry David a little. They could hardly hope to walk away from the Sioux. They might get away from the camp, but in the end the Indians would be able to track them all too easily. The Sioux had the horses, too.

Nate stirred beside him. He touched David's hand with his own to tell him he had found and now held a sturdy rock. David shook his head. A rock would be useless.

They lay for a long time in uncomfortable silence. The moon now shone out of the south. The whippoorwills had ceased to call. A few owls still shattered the darkness with their weird calls now and then. The Sioux lay motionless, breathing evenly. For all that, David knew that they slept very lightly.

He put his mouth to Nate's ear and whispered, "I'm going."

Then he began to inch around the scrub growth. He went with infinite caution, careful to make only the most minute sounds. Fortunately, there were no dry leaves and no sticks in his path. Very slowly, he pulled himself forward on hands and knees, until he was directly behind the tree to which Suydam was tied.

He reached up, hesitantly. What if Suydam cried out? He must take that chance. He patted Suydam's bound hands. Suydam's fingers responded. He pressed Suydam's hands reassuringly, and at once began to cut at the thongs with his knife. He had to feel his way with his fingers, for the back of the tree was in deep shadow.

In a little while Suydam's hands were free. Cutting the thongs that bound his legs took but a moment more.

For a long minute nothing happened. Suydam was flexing his hands. Then he stood on tiptoe several times. David had begun to draw back, as soon as he had freed Suydam.

Then Suydam stepped quietly forward, picked up his gun, and slipped behind the tree. David beckoned him to follow.

They began to creep noiselessly away from the Sioux camp, foot by foot. It seemed to David a long way until they reached the scrub growth which had sheltered him.

Then, with Nate, they crept back the way they had come. The light of the moon helped a little, but not much. The woods were not too dense, but the leaves shut away most of the moonlight.

They drew slowly away from the Sioux camp. Soon they did not have to be so cautious. Yet even so, none of them made any sound. And no one trusted himself to speak.

They rose to their feet, still moving slowly and with care because the lack of light did not encourage them to go faster lest they blunder into something and arouse the camp behind them.

Not until they reached the place where David and Nate

had left the main trail made by the horses did they stop to talk. Even then, it was but in whispers.

"Hold up," said Suydam. "We're three against three, if the worst comes."

"Mr. Suydam, we'll have to keep moving," said David earnestly. "They'll try to find you again."

"I don't know. Only the one of them claimed me. The others took my instruments. The one intended—as far as I could guess—to use me for something when they got back into the west. They were heading out of the Territory, and the one seemed to be bound for the tribe. The others weren't going back with the one who claimed me."

"He was going to use you for a trade," said David. "We'll have to go on."

"We can't see well enough in the dark," objected Nate.

"Besides, I'm just too tired, David—I'm sorry. We'll have to think of something else. Look—I remember we passed through a woods of old trees—or just along the edge of it."

"That's not far away," said David.

"Well, then, come on—we'll get to that." He started away, adding, "Be careful not to leave any more trail than you can help. Use the old trail all the way."

They reached the woods. There Suydam paused again, looking around him by the light of the moon.

"Now, then—there's an old tree. By jumping, we might just catch hold of that limb. Up we go!"

Suydam jumped first. On the second try, he got hold of the limb. David and Nate supported him until he got a good hold and could pull himself up. Then they handed the guns up to him.

It was David's turn next. Suydam helped pull him up.

Last came Nate.

"Now what?" asked David.

"This is where we stay for the night. If they follow, we have the advantage of being able to blow them to kingdom come—if we have to. I'd just as soon not—that might bring a hornet's nest on us, if there are any others around. But I don't think there are. These renegades seem to be the only human beings in this country.

"Now crawl over to the trunk and make yourselves as comfortable as you can. Try to get some sleep. You'll be paddling tomorrow—while I rest. The minute we get back, we're for home!"

Just before dawn, Suydam awakened David and Nate. Despite the discomfort of their positions, the boys had managed to sleep a few hours. Now, however, the grimness of their position was brought home to them by the first words Suydam spoke.

"Take your guns and climb up a little higher—out of sight. The Sioux will be awake now, and we'll find out whether they intend to hunt us down."

The amber glow in the east turned to peach, then to a lambent old rose, then to a brilliant orange. The sun pushed into the sky from the dark rim of earth. The three of them waited.

The sun was not yet free of the horizon when Suydam made a small sound of warning. David looked quickly to the trail from among the leaves. Far to the west—he judged it to be at that place where they had left the horse's trail—a single Indian was following the way they had come.

Suydam motioned to the boys to make ready, but not to

fire until they were sure it was necessary. Then he crawled out on the limb above the trail and waited.

The Sioux came on, rapidly, his eyes to the ground. They had left marks, David knew, which he could read. The Indian came on like a hunting dog. Soon he was at the edge of the wood, following the path which led beneath the tree.

He passed under the tree and stopped. David almost gasped. The Sioux could see the jump mark Suydam had made when he failed to reach the limb overhead the first time.

But before the Indian could look up, Suydam acted. He swung the stock of his gun in an arc and struck the Sioux a hard blow on the back of his head. His action was so violent that his gun flew out of his hands and he himself tumbled from the limb. But the Sioux had fallen, and Suydam fell on top of him, unhurt.

David and Nate came down the tree like squirrels.

"I hate to kill anyone if I don't have to," explained Suydam. "He'll be knocked out for some time. We'll tie him up and leave him. By the time his friends begin to look for him, we'll be well on our way."

Suydam took off his shirt and tore it into strips.

They tied the Sioux securely, then gagged him. When they had finished, they carried him back into the woods a short distance and left him there.

"If they find him, well and good—he'll have lost face," said Suydam. "If they don't—he can free himself, I think. We know where we stand now—only one of them wants me. Let's go."

They set off in a rapid, loping trot, back along the trail the two boys had followed so carefully the day before. The sun was as hot, and the mosquitoes as troublesome, but somehow their tiredness did not seem to matter. All that counted was to put as much distance between them and the Sioux camp as possible. Nor did the pangs of hunger bother them, for a greater urgency impelled them to hurry.

They made better time than they had made the previous day. For one thing, they did not have to take care lest someone hear or see them. For another, the trail now had a kind of familiarity.

When at last they reached the rust-colored river, the boys could have shouted for joy. But Suydam did not pause. He turned north at once and moved fast along the path David and Nate had followed to the place where the Indians had captured him.

At noon they reached the place of their camp. The canoe was just as they had left it.

Though they were tired and hungry, they did not lose a moment in uncovering the canoe and snaking it into the water.

Then they started down the river for the long pull back to Detroit.

XV.

HOME AGAIN

IT WAS SEPTEMBER when they reached Detroit.
The journey back through Lake Superior to the Sault—
from that northernmost post to Mackinac—and from the
Island of the Turtle down through Lake Huron along the
eastern boundary of the Michigan Territory—had taken
longer than they counted on because of many delays for repair of their canoe as well as the need to stop and hunt along
shore—and much stormier weather than they had met on the
trip out.

But now they were back. The city teemed, as they remembered it, with settlers coming in from the east. David and
Nate did not recognize a familiar face as they pushed through
the crowds.

They made their way directly to Governor Mason's house.

The Governor was not at home, but the old housekeeper welcomed them like long-lost relatives. "The Governor's been expectin' ye this long time," she cried. "Two months!" She shook her head, as if to condemn their delay. "He'll be home to dinner. I'll send word to him. Ye're to wait now— and don't go off."

The Governor hurried home as soon as the message from his housekeeper reached him. He had been with the Legislative Council. He was thinner than David last recalled him, and he looked unwell, but he was as full of energy as always.

"I thought we'd lost you," he said as he came in. "How did you find our Territory, Mr. Suydam?"

"A very rich land, sir."

Governor Mason smiled triumphantly. "Haven't I always said so! But you'll be making a formal report—and perhaps you've lived with your findings for so long there's no need to go over them here. You'll all have dinner with me, of course."

He turned and shouted toward the kitchen. "Martha! Company for dinner!"

"Right soon, sir!" came the answer from the kitchen.

The Governor sat down. "It's good to rest a little. I've not been well."

"How's the war, sir?" asked David.

Governor Mason chuckled. "The casualties have been very moderate. Perhaps a dozen pigs—a score of poultry—and two horses, one on each side." He laughed. "It's been a war of writs and words and fists—and all the gunfire's been so bad you'd think nobody on either side ever held a gun before!

"We did arrest one of the Ohioans—a Major Stickney. The men tied him to his horse and forced him to ride to Monroe. Such a fooferaw! The Governor of Ohio accused us of kidnapping one of his citizens. And the men on both sides got out of hand—broke into a few houses and ruined the press of the Toledo *Gazette*. But not so much as a bullet wound has anyone got!"

"Is it over, sir?" asked Nate.

"I'd say it is. We've reached a stalemate. Our militia is still down there. So is Ohio's. Ohio stole a march on us early this month, when they sneaked into Toledo one midnight and held court there for a few minutes. Then they ran out again. That gives them a certain advantage—they exercised jurisdiction, we can't deny that—and Washington is bound to take notice of it."

"It'll count for Ohio," said Suydam.

"I know. But we haven't been idle. We've had a caucus here for statehood. We've nominated Isaac Crary for Congress, and the men have done me the honor to nominate me for the first Governor of the new State of Michigan."

"But will they recognize the caucus in Washington?" asked Suydam.

"No. Nor the election—not right away. The election's bound to follow—they can't stop us. But in the end they will recognize us—they will—and Michigan will join the Union in its rightful role as a new State."

"And the Toledo War, sir?" asked David. "Will we win it? I mean about the land we were quarrelling about . . ."

Governor Mason's face clouded. "That remains to be seen. I hear rumors from Washington that they incline to favor

Ohio. They plan instead to offer us that frozen waste of the peninsula."

Suydam leaned forward. "Well, sir, that's most interesting. I'd take their offer."

"Why do you say that?"

"Because that's no frozen waste, Governor."

"How can you say that, Suydam?"

"We were there."

The Governor's eyes lit with surprise. "You were on the peninsula!" he exclaimed. "I thought you'd confine yourselves to the area this side of Lake Michigan."

"We had orders to survey the Michigan Territory. We had no orders to stop short of the peninsula. We traded off our horses for a canoe and took the old fur-trading route along the south shore of Lake Superior. Far from being a frozen waste, the land to the northwest is rich in timber. What's more—and perhaps even more important for Michigan's future—there are definite traces of iron and copper."

Governor Mason's face broke into a broad smile. His eyes twinkled with pleasure. "Well, that puts an entirely different complexion on the matter," he said. "Do you think many people in Washington might be aware of that knowledge?"

"It's hard to say, sir."

"I think our statehood is as good as granted. We'll stall them and back away from their offer for a while—that will make them only the more insistent. Then we'll give in—let Ohio have the Toledo strip and take the peninsula."

"The peninsula is far more valuable than the Toledo strip, Governor," said Suydam. "It's so much larger an area, to begin with—wildly beautiful, with many rivers—and I'm con-

vinced the mineral deposits are far greater than the samples
I found have led me to suspect. But you'll see them—and
you'll have my report soon."

"I look forward to it with an eagerness I can hardly sup-
press," answered the Governor. He turned to David and Nate.
"Now for the boys," he went on. "We can use young men
who aren't afraid to take chances. I can find places for both
of you here in Detroit."

"I'll take that offer, thank you, sir," answered Nate
promptly.

David held back. Now that he was faced with the choice,
he hesitated. Now he could go on to greater adventures. Was
this not why he had left the farm in the first place? He had
been tired of farm life—but he was not so any longer. Besides,
he needn't be in a hurry to make a decision. He had proved
himself. He could always accept the Governor's offer.

"Well, David?" asked Governor Mason.

"Sir, I don't know," answered David. "I'd have to think it
over. I've seen something of the world now, and I can see
that the farmer in the wilderness is the backbone of the country, if you come right down to it. I think, sir, I'd rather go
back to the farm—for now. Some day perhaps I'll own a farm
of my own."

Governor Mason smiled understandingly. "My offer is
always open, David. You'll want to go home then?"

"Yes, sir."

"You'll stay the night?"

"No, sir. I plan to set out right after dinner."

"I'll see to it that your pay's ready for you. And if the
time comes when you want a farm of your own—or a hanker-

ing to try for new adventures—come to see me and we'll talk it over."

Nate moistened his lips eagerly. "Sir, there's nothing I'd like better than farming."

Governor Mason laughed. "I think you'll get over it, Nate. Try it for a while. You'll soon see you're either born to it or you're not. David's born to it."

"Nate'll come and spend a while with us after he's seen his folks," said David.

The housekeeper came bustling in to say that dinner was ready and waiting.

It was almost evening when David came within sight of the little clearing where the Claver homestead stood. This time there was no one outside to see him come. They were in the house, eating supper.

How good everything looked! As he walked along, David took account of every field. He saw how much more land Pa and Willie had cleared. He saw that the fence had been extended, making the farm look bigger than ever. His palms began to itch with eagerness to get back to the work he had done for so long.

He paused a moment outside the house.

There was still time to turn back. But there would always be time for a resolute man to make a change, and his time was not yet.

When he stepped toward the warm glow of the kitchen, David knew that he would be home once more—home to the farm—and soon, perhaps, to a farm of his own. A man always had the choice of whether to live close to the good earth or apart from it.

He walked around to the back door and threw it open.
Ma looked at him with opened mouth and wide eyes.
Willie spun around and shouted, "Davie!"
Pa turned slowly and met his glance.
"Pa, I'm home," said David.